THE RAID ON THE VILLA JOYOSA

The Raid on the Villa Joyosa

by ROBERT HOPKINS

G. P. Putnam's Sons
New York

Copyright © 1973 by Robert Hopkins

All rights reserved. This book, or parts thereof, must not be reproduced in any form without permission. Published simultaneously in Canada by Longman Canada Limited, Toronto.

SBN: 399-11111-5

Library of Congress Catalog
Card Number: 72-97310

PRINTED IN THE UNITED STATES OF AMERICA

THE RAID ON THE VILLA JOYOSA

1

It took me exactly three seconds to confirm what I had known all along. The accountants are taking over the bloody world.

The name plaque on his desk looked like a bad draw at Scrabble. "H. R. F. Quinn," it said, with "ACA" after it in smaller letters.

Half-moon spectacles balanced on a long, thin nose, hair Brylcreamed into a carapace, and that extra layer of politeness the Brits get when they think they've got you by the short hairs.

I wasn't having any of it, not the way I felt.

"An extension to five hundred pounds should do nicely, Mr. Quinn," I said, getting straight to the point.

"I should think so, Mr. Begay," Quinn replied, a smile as thin as a razor blade fixed on his bland face.

He sat hunched behind a wide leather-topped desk, his hands folded neatly in the center of a large green desk blotter. The blotter was without a smudge that I could see.

There was a long silence while I stared at Quinn and he stared at me. I couldn't afford the wait.

"If you'd rather I discuss it with the director, I perfectly understand," I said. "My letter was addressed to the director."

Quinn didn't even blink. "Well, ah, yes. Since these matters are my bailiwick, he asked me to speak with you."

I didn't like the oily way he'd slid over "these matters," but I was started, and there was nothing to do but brazen it out. "Then if you'll approve the credit extension, Mr. Quinn, there'll be no need to trouble anyone further."

"No trouble really, Mr. Begay. But there are one or two items we should attend to first, if you don't mind."

Before I could say I'd rather not, he lifted a mud-brown legal-size folder from the middle desk drawer, watching me all the while over the bottom half of his glasses. He put the folder carefully in front of him.

Lettered in a neat feminine hand across a gummed label at the top was "Samuel Osmond Begay." For no apparent reason there was an exclamation point after it.

My stomach began to get a familiar, nasty feeling.

"In fact, if you hadn't visited us," Quinn went on, "we most likely would have taken pains to contact you. Our inquiry into your case has brought to light quite a number of things."

"My case?" He made it sound like the bloody Royal College of Surgeons.

Quinn smiled wide enough to show the space between his front teeth. "A gaming club of our stature must be quite careful of its membership. Gaming Board regulations, you understand."

I understood. "I'm afraid we'll have to discuss it another time, Mr. Quinn. I have rather a full afternoon ahead of me." I rose to go.

"Do you really?" said Quinn, smiling mirthlessly. "I was under the impression you had nothing to do whatsoever, this afternoon or any other afternoon for that matter. Sit down, Mr. Begay." He pointed to the chair, the politeness peeling off his voice like cheap enamel. "By the time you leave this office I intend to have this affair settled one way or the other."

I sat down and wondered if Quinn could hear my teeth grinding. He went on twittering.

"You have opened this Pandora's box, so to speak, and we have been forced to look into it. We haven't liked what we have found." He cleared his throat and glanced at the folder. "Item one. You owe us three hundred and forty-seven pounds and fifty new pence. According to bylaw nine, regular members are forbidden to exceed the statutory limit of credit, which I need not remind you is three hundred pounds."

"I enclosed a check for fifty pounds in the letter requesting the extension of credit."

"Yes," said Quinn tonelessly. "Which brings us to item two. The Melbury Court branch of Barclays advised me, informally of course, that you have an overdraft exceeding seven hundred pounds. They were reluctant to allow it to increase before having a word with you. It seems they no longer have your current address."

It was even worse than I thought. "Informally" was the key word. I began to smell a typical accountants' conspiracy brewing away in the back room. I told Quinn I'd certainly have a talk with my bank manager about that.

"Yes, you must do," he said evenly. "I'm afraid that still leaves us with this." He extracted my check from the folder and fluttered it at me. "I wonder if you might possibly make it good." His voice was suddenly cheerful, the tit.

"Now?"

"If you please."

"I seldom carry large amounts of cash with me."

"We'll accept whatever amount you have."

Like bloody hell. I gave him five quid, which was half of my total liquid assets anyway. He put the check carefully back into the folder. I waited while he wrote out a receipt.

Then he moved the specs around on his nose, shuffled through the papers in the file, and said, ah, yes. "That brings us to item three."

I wasn't going to wait for it. "We've gone far enough, Mr. Quinn. I came here for a little service, which I think you'll agree is a member's due. . . ."

"You came here to stretch the privileges of club membership to the limit, Mr. Begay, a membership given you in good faith and which we may very well revoke." He spread both hands on the desk and leaned toward me. "You may leave if you care to. In which case the matter is closed. Or you may, according to bylaw eighteen, appeal the recommendation of the membership committee, of which I am chairman. In that instance you had best refute the validity of the information I have gathered here." He poked the folder with a finger like a quill. "The choice is yours."

It didn't sound like a choice to me. "I'm prepared to correct any misinformation you may have gathered, Mr. Quinn."

He began to smile thinly again. "An appropriate choice of words, Mr. Begay. I have no doubt we have been misinformed about you. Your original application for membership is a case in point."

I put as much contempt as I could into a grunt, but I was trying to remember exactly what I'd said on the application. Despite all that guff about standards, I'd never seen a gaming club yet that checked beyond your ability to cough up six guineas a year and keep the chips sliding across the tables. Not unless they sensed the flailings of a drowning man. I did tend to be rather extravagant describing my past accomplishments. I mean we're all the same, aren't we?

"You stated your occupation as chef." Quinn's faint smile turned malicious. "And your place of employment the Mirabelle."

The truth had suddenly spread itself very thin. "At that time absolutely correct," I said, and added what seemed to me just the right touch of upmanship: "I've since accepted another position."

Quinn made a small *ah* of satisfaction. His head began to waggle slowly from side to side. "Quite incorrect."

It was time to be quiet.

"You were never a chef at the Mirabelle, Mr. Begay."

My stomach felt as though I'd been sipping kerosene. "A matter of professional terminology."

His head continued to waggle. "For a brief period you prepared salads at a restaurant named Chez Mirabelle, a hostelry of quite a different order."

"I omitted the Chez. A human mistake."

"Mistake, Mr. Begay? I can assure you the management

of even Chez Mirabelle feels precisely the same way. Your length of employment was exactly four days."

"We didn't get along."

"You were fired for incompetence."

"Now what did you expect them to say?"

Quinn's fingers danced on the desk. "Sometime, Mr. Begay, I would like to learn exactly how one fails totally in the preparation of lettuce and tomatoes."

I knew, but I didn't say anything.

Quinn leaned forward, his eyes a pair of large gray disks in the lenses. It was as though he were seeing me for the first time. "You're not British, are you?"

He said it as if it were the explanation for everything.

"I'm an American citizen, if it's any concern of yours."

"The background of our members is very much my concern, Mr. Begay. I find your accent rather odd even for an American."

I didn't feel like explaining to Quinn the fat difference between holding American citizenship and being American. My mother was American, my father French. From the age of nine on I'd been raised largely in France by an uncle I grew up calling Papa. What I knew about the United States was a blurry memory of a piece of turf from Bronx Zoo to the Battery and the kind of mishmash you learn about a place from its movies. I could have told Quinn more about John Wayne on the Rio Bravo than Washington at Valley Forge. It wouldn't have got me anywhere. To Quinn, any accent that wasn't Oxford or Cambridge was suspect.

"I was born in New York City," I said, and let it go at that.

"Yes. So the Metropolitan Police informed me. At least that much is true."

"The police?"

"The Alien Registration Section, actually. I had a word with them regarding you. Informally, of course."

"I'll bet."

"Their records indicate an employer other than either of the Mirabelles."

He named a hotel on Basil Street I'd worked at so many jobs ago it barely remained in my memory. I'd planned to have my Certificate of Registration amended when I settled into something permanent. I still did.

Quinn was droning on, enjoying every word. "May I remind you, Mr. Begay, that since you are no longer employed at that establishment, you are in violation of the Alien Order of 1953. As you know, all resident aliens are required to notify the police of any change of address or employment. At this moment, if given reason to press it, you would be subject to expulsion."

"You've reminded me. I'll take care of it."

He looked surprised. "Then you are employed?"

"Of course I'm employed."

"Might I ask where?"

He could have found out informally from one of his underground anyway. Besides, there was nothing outwardly disreputable about the Fleur de Lis. I told him what I did and where.

A satisfied look spread across Quinn's face. "A waiter. That's quite a comedown from, ah, chef."

"Nothing like keeping your hand on the public tastes, so to speak." I tried to keep it light, but the words rasped from a throat gone suddenly dry.

His head started moving again. "Really, that will never do. In view of the unfortunate circumstances, Mr. Begay, I'm afraid we must withdraw your membership." His satisfied look turned nasty. "Effective immediately."

"It's people like you, Quinn, who make unfortunate circumstances."

"I beg your pardon?"

"And don't give me that we business, you mealy wank. I'll bet there *isn't* a membership committee." I was on my feet now.

Quinn's complexion went pasty.

"I urge you to remain businesslike, Mr. Begay. There is still the matter of your debt to be settled."

I told him where he could stuff his businesslike manner and the debt.

"I warned you, Mr. Begay."

"Why do you think I joined this ruddy place? To pay my debts, that's why."

"That's entirely your concern," said Quinn, his eyes beginning to jerk around.

"They close down Crockfords and leave a bloody trap like this open. It's a shame. And don't think I haven't seen a share of seconds dealt around the twenty-one table either."

Quinn began to look frightened. "Insults will not make this easier, Mr. Begay." A hand disappeared beneath the desk.

"But it makes me feel better, and that's no small thing these days." I had six inches' height on Quinn, and a good twenty pounds. I was measuring the distance across the green desk blotter to Quinn's old school tie when I heard the door open behind me and close with a click.

I turned around. The space in the room had suddenly been reduced by half.

"Everything all right, Mr. Quinn?" said the mountain occupying the other half.

"Mr. Begay was just leaving, Armstrong. Perhaps you'll show him the door."

Armstrong. It was like naming a burglar Mr. Crook. Maybe Quinn had a sense of humor after all.

2

"Be a good boy," Armstrong said, putting me into a taxi. He waved good-bye.

I gave him the horns through the taxi window and told the cabby the address of the Fleur de Lis. "And hurry."

His eyes gave me a snotty "you must be joking" look in the rearview, but when he saw the expression on my face, they snapped straight ahead. He pushed the taxi into the rush-hour traffic caterpillaring west along Oxford Street, then cut north through Paddington to miss the usual hopeless snarl at Marble Arch.

I'd lose twenty minutes taking a cab, and I was already late. I wasn't in shape to ride the tube in any case. I could feel the sweat standing out on my forehead, and my stomach had knotted itself around a burning lump of coal.

Quinn's remark about the comedown from chef to waiter had opened the wound. Thanks to the help of a straight-talking analyst named Manning Able, I'd only recently admitted to myself I was a failure in the kitchen. I wasn't ready to admit it to Quinn. If Papa Victor had known I'd ended up working as a waiter, he'd have swiveled in his grave like a dervish.

The males on my father's side of the family have all been chefs, extraordinary ones. My father was an assistant at the Plaza in New York City. His brother, my uncle Victor, was *gros bonnet* to some of the best restaurants and hotels in Europe, including the Grand in Monte Carlo under Prosper Montagné. I was practically raised in the kitchen and naturally had expected to follow along in the family footsteps, which definitely never ventured among the riffraff.

Papa Victor sensed I was the victim of a recessive gene even before I did. I was eighteen at the time, serving a rather protracted apprenticeship under him at the Reno in Barcelona. I'd been working over an oeufs Omer Pasha and was just finishing the onion puree when I looked up and found him standing over me, examining my work. I don't know if it is possible to look sad and disgusted at the same time, but the look on his face should have been a warning. He'd always told me you were born with the talent for *haute cuisine*. His face said it clearly: I did not have it. I was the kitchen equivalent of a color-blind painter or tone-deaf musician.

While he was alive, I considered Papa Victor the chief irritant in my life. He was a nasty-mouthed bear of a man, who ate too much, and drank too much, and had a lot of other excesses that finally caught up with him. He died, happily I'm told, in a very good house in Marseilles, between the thighs of an Algerian-Chinese girl named Mina. When he was gone, I missed him.

But for reasons I'd only recently begun to understand I ignored his warning. I wasted a lot of good years talking my way into one kitchen after another, trading on a fat theoretical knowledge about food and cooking, hoping for the talent to gel.

"A rather simple delusion of desire," Manning Able had explained to me pleasantly, as though my prolonged flight of fancy hadn't already complicated my life. "In your case slightly morbid. These recent impulses to punish yourself aren't at all uncommon, considering." His eyelids fluttered shut, then blinked open, and he very nearly smiled. "A good thing in one way. It means you've avoided becoming a full-blown paranoid." We both laughed at that, although I wasn't sure what I was laughing about.

I'd telephoned Manning Able the first morning I'd walked out of Westminster Hospital, after my nine-year-old Morgan had wandered across the center median near Hyde Park Corner and climbed an aluminum light standard. The resident surgeon who put fourteen stitches in my chin didn't believe the car had done it on its own. Neither did I, really. Manning Able was the first name on a list of psychiatrists I had the doctor write out for me.

It had taken fifteen sessions, talks he preferred to call them, in brightly lit rooms in a Victorian town house on Wimpole Street before I began to get an inkling of my problem.

"Your subconscious fixed on the goal of becoming a great chef, which was perfectly understandable given your family and early environment. When you began to realize it was beyond you, subconsciously you experienced a sense of guilt and began to devise ways to punish yourself for failure. Your compulsive gambling, the accident, who knows what else. It's nonsense, of course. You're a nice-looking boy, Samuel. You have health, and women aren't the problem. Under those circumstances there's no such thing as a twenty-eight-year-old failure, unless you want to be."

"That's what you say."

"That's what I know." His eyelids fluttered, and he smiled.

He was a small man, dark and dapper, who looked in his mid-fifties. I found out later he wasn't a Brit at all, but Czech and a little over seventy. He'd won a chestful of medals flying for the RAF in 1940 and '41, until an air crash had fused the lower half of his spine and a few other things. When he walked, it made you uncomfortable to watch.

"Why can't I do it, Manning?"

"Become a master chef? Why not a virtuoso on the violin? It's the same question. Certain things in this world take a specific talent, and no one, my dear Samuel, knows why some have it and others do not. In the kitchen you apparently don't, and you know it. Otherwise you wouldn't be here." He shrugged stiffly, the palms of his small hands turning upward. "You could cook, just as you could play the violin. Obviously, doing either poorly doesn't interest you."

I nodded and asked, "But why so long to own up to it?"

"Some people never face the idea they should have done something else with their lives. The path of least resistance from cradle to grave." One small hand made a toboggan swoop toward the wastebasket. "Besides, you're a stubborn young man. That stomach of yours is still holding out."

"My ulcer?"

Manning Able shook his head. "It's not an ulcer, Samuel. Somatization we call it. It's a defense mechanism of a bruised ego. If you had wanted to play the piano, it would be stiff fingers. The pains will go when you straighten yourself out."

"And when does that happen?"

His eyelids flickered and he smiled. "You might resolve things with a couple of years' expensive analysis. If you were a middle-aged stockbroker who suddenly decided he might have been happier as a wicketkeeper, I'd recommend it." The eyes closed, but the smile remained. "It helps, sometimes."

"I can't afford it either way. Time and money I'm running out of."

"You don't need analysis, Samuel. At least not yet." The eyelids fluttered open, and his bright eyes stared at me, and a little beyond. "Just make a success of something your fat ego can live with."

"Is that all?"

He made a tired sigh. "I'm afraid you're one of those unfortunate souls with a compulsion to take bigger bites of life than they can chew. If you could be happy with the modest or mediocre, it would be better for you. Such people are inclined to be happy."

"And what if I don't find this big something?"

"Stay out of automobiles," Manning said.

I started to laugh, but it's no fun laughing by yourself. Manning Able sat watching me, a concerned human being staring out through his professional manner.

"And you had better come back and see me," he added. I started to say something but he held up his hand. "At that point, we won't worry about money."

But I did worry about money. Constantly. Manning Able hadn't given me a clue how I was supposed to keep mind and body together while my ego found something to pacify itself. The only business I knew was food, and there wasn't a restaurateur in London willing to risk his clientele with me in the kitchen. When I walked into the labor exchange on Denmark Street these days, I was welcomed like meningitis.

I'd thought about changing addresses, trying the Midlands, maybe even the States. But I've tried to change my luck by moving before. The same old Begay always tags along.

Working as a waiter was a natural move, the path of least resistance as Manning had called it. With what I knew about food, it wasn't hard to develop a flashy kind of competence, like those second-rate entertainers you see with all the moves and gestures a little too slick, to make up for the real talent that's missing. Faking it wasn't easy to live with.

By the time the taxi had weaved its way as far as the top of Queensway, my stomach had wound itself up like a watchspring.

The Fleur de Lis was in a neighborhood of Indian delis and fourth-rate hotels and tobacco shops that turned a neat penny displaying the blank side of postcards with inviting little messages written on them: "Unemployed French model seeks unusual new position. Phone Miss Coucher." Or "Strict German governess will give riding lessons to precocious pupils." All with phone numbers nearby. The best most Londoners would say about the neighborhood was "improving," in that odd way the Brits have of putting a thing down while still managing to say something nice about it. But from June through September the whole area swarmed with tourists. That's what Parakis, the owner of the Fleur de Lis, was after. Him and everyone else.

Not that the restaurant was a tourist trap by design. Parakis thought he ran an authentic bistro, *très intime*. Rough tablecloths, Duralex crockery, and Piaf and Aznavour squawking breathlessly from the Muzak. The menu was very French, handwritten in purple ink and completely indecipherable. Of course the chef was a Sicilian who just might have known the difference between *crevette* and *cravate*, the other four waiters were Spaniards, and Parakis was a nasty-tempered Greek Cypriot who had hired me because he was a raving Francophile and wanted to practice his bad French. "You give the place a little class, Sammy," he said. *"Une ambiance continentale."*

It occurred to me at that point Manning Able was right. To work in the Fleur de Lis, I had to be punishing myself for something.

I had the cabby let me off a little past the entrance and paid him off, giving him a larger toke than I should have. Driving a taxicab is a grunt business, I figure.

I went in the back door, grabbed my uniform jacket off the hook, and made it into the men's without anyone seeing me, I thought.

Neil walked in a second later. "Do you have it?" he asked flatly.

I gave him a look that said I thought he was pigeonshit on a windowsill, but it didn't do any good. He asked me again. "Do you, or don't you?"

"No," I said. "I'll pay you tomorrow."

"Don't be cheeky, Sammy. You promised. Ten for twelve, one day only. We agreed."

"All I have is five."

"I'll take the five." I gave him the change from the taxi. "This is only four pounds forty pence." He rolled his eyes back and looked at the ceiling.

Neil thought of himself as a maître d'. In a place the

caliber of the Fleur de Lis all he did in actual fact was show people to their table in a swish fashion, which Neil was very good at. His hair was poofed, feathered, and tipped. He wore those skintight peekaboo shirts that look right only on slender, hairless people. But anyone who made the mistake of guessing Neil was a powder puff paid for it in scar tissue.

He watched me change clothes.

"You haven't got the word, have you, Neil?"

"About what?"

"Hairy chests are coming back."

"The money, Sammy."

"I said I'd get it."

"When?" He took advantage of the mirror and gave his layered hair a fluff.

"It's only seven quid, Neil."

"It's seven pounds sixty pence." He smoothed his eyebrows and wetted his pink lips. "You'd better be very smooth tonight, Sammy." He gave me a vicious sneer, spun on his platform heels, and left.

If there was anything more potentially dangerous than a poovy loan shark, I couldn't think what it was.

I snapped on my bow tie and headed for the garret.

When I went through the main dining room, the Spaniards were standing around with their hands behind their backs, dark and slender, looking very much like the vultures they were.

Parakis glowered at me over the top of the cash register, his eyebrows so close together it looked as though someone had painted a black stripe above his eyes. There were only three tables occupied, so I judged that was part of it.

The whole restaurant had eighty-five chairs, sixteen tables for four on the main floor, plus some postage stamps with legs rammed in the odd space. I'd been the last waiter hired, which meant I had the pleasure of working the garret, a small room up three stairs and off to the left of the main dining room.

In it were four tables, a total of sixteen places, which

I had yet to fill and empty once a night. In the garret I had plenty of chance to think, which I didn't necessarily want.

Mechanically I went through my nightly preparations. I respaced the tables so at two of them my clients at least had enough room to move their elbows. Then I unplugged the fan which Parakis put in thinking he was doing everyone a favor. That fan would put a chill on any hot dish in two seconds flat and played havoc with the occasional dish I had to flame. With everything else the Fleur de Lis' patrons were likely to have against them, it was the least I could do.

The hustle was Neil's idea, but the truth is I didn't object. Everything that happened at the Fleur de Lis seemed to take place in a vacuum. It was as though time were suspended, and when it would begin again, I couldn't have told anyone. Neil's hustle shouldn't have bothered me at all. I knew for a fact Parakis refilled the empties of first-class French wines with Spanish and Algerian plonk. The Spaniards inflated tabs as a matter of habit and would try anything they could get away with without Parakis seeing them. In such an atmosphere of blatant crookery it was easy to go along with the motto Parakis must have had lettered on his shaving mirror: "Honesty is not getting caught."

Double counting currency is a fairly common hustle of vendors and carnies, and when Neil showed me the trick, I learned it without any trouble.

"Look, Sammy," he explained, standing a little too close for comfort. "Whenever you get the chance, all you have to do is count out the change, double counting one of those bills the way I showed you. I'll steer attractive marks to the garret, and we split fifty-fifty."

"Me taking one hundred percent of the risk."

"Honestly, Sammy." I expected him to stamp his foot.

"What if someone just happens to notice?"

He looked at me as though the answer were the most obvious thing in the world. "Sammy, who is going to notice a little thing like that when they've had a few? Most of the people that come into the Fleur de Lis are practically *pleading* with someone to take their money. Besides, the mark sees you count the right change, doesn't he? Psychologically it's almost foolproof. I have it on good advice."

"But just say someone counts his change again and finds he's one bill short?"

Neil smiled triumphantly. "You made a mistake. That's all you have to say. The odds are one in a million." He gave my arm a tentative squeeze. "Don't tell me you couldn't use a little extra scratch?"

Considering the amount of money I watched disappear across the twenty-one table nightly, I couldn't argue. Manning Able hadn't let me get away with it, though. He thought agreeing to such a scuddy con was nothing but the punishment business again. As it turned out, he was dead right.

When I'd finished refolding the napkins, I was ready for the evening to begin.

Up to a point I remember that night very clearly, in a way anyone might who had a chance to watch his own funeral. It was a Tuesday, which in the restaurant business can be deadly. It was also the first day in June that gave any indication that summer might grace London at all. The air had a warm, lazy feel that made you want to curl up with someone you liked, and not in a restaurant either.

By ten o'clock I'd served eight dinners.

I'd had one party of four, all gray-haired octogenarians wearing plastic name cards, warning me ahead of time they were on a "Golden Years" holiday. They completely ignored the "service non compris" stamped in bright red across the bottom of the tab and left me twelve new pence. But they were a cheery lot, and I didn't mind. It was nice to know you could live that long and still find things to be cheery about.

Then came a young couple, stiff and overdressed, honeymooners for sure. They pinched each other under the table, cooing in German, which is not easy to do. The mark didn't even notice when I double counted a quid, the one I'd already lifted from his change safely in my pocket.

Two Japanese gentlemen dangling cameras like infantry equipment picked at truite amandine until they thought it must be all right. Then they ate it heads and all. They counted their change carefully and ended up leaving me a quid. It was about twice what they should have.

By then it was almost eleven. Losing my club membership meant I was for the time being barred from the arena with Dame Fortune. Maybe it was a good thing. T. I. T. Quinn's nasty reminder of the money I owed wasn't a good thing. I had two quid twelve pence worth of tokes in my pocket, and I'd had to steal half of that. The money blues settled on me like the pox. The walls of the garret shrank to the dimensions of a steamer trunk, and that familiar nasty feeling I lived with like a sick relative crawled into my stomach and stayed there.

It was then Neil walked in escorting the three of them.

3

The truth is I didn't know what to make of them. This trio weren't the usual tourists that wandered into the Fleur de Lis. My eyes should have opened right then.

The first man was dressed a little too well. Pale well-cut tropical suit, expensive shirt. He was about my height but lean, so that he looked taller than he was. Too lean and tight for an ordinary businessman. And down deep a tenseness that gave you the impression if he took off his jacket he'd uncoil in about six different directions at once, which wasn't too far from wrong. He looked about twenty-two or -three, but I found out later he was closer my age. That turned out to be Howard, of course.

The second man was another type altogether. Pushing middle age and had made the decision twenty pounds ago to wear his belt beneath the bulge of stomach. He was a stump with legs. His shirt collar was open around a thick neck, exposing one of those furry chests that looked as though it would have engulfed his whole neck and face if it weren't forced down periodically with a sharp razor.

By himself I might have pegged him for an oil or construction worker straight in from Cabinda or the Arabian Gulf, spoiling for a lot of booze and some whoring around.

He pulled out the chair for the girl who didn't fit that order at all, although I'm the first to admit that these days you can't tell by looking.

She was leggy and slender-hipped, with the slenderness

filling out under the top of an emerald-green sheath dress. Her honey-colored hair was worn long and slightly wild. She looked about twenty or twenty-one and settled on the chair with a lightness that wouldn't have cracked an egg.

"Bring us some cee-gars," the stump said. He turned to Neil and peeled off a blue five-pound note. "Good ones. And see not too many people interrupt us. We got business to talk."

His accent was American, straight out of the woods, a drawling countrified voice that went with the open face. He didn't sound overly bright.

On the way out Neil gave me a grin as if he were about to seduce his first thirteen-year-old.

I scooped up three menus and attacked.

The young one in the light suit glanced over the menu quickly and looked up. His eyes took me in with one sweep. They were without expression, except when they settled on me I had the disturbing feeling they were looking inside my skull.

"What's your name?" he asked quietly.

"Samuel."

"Samuel, we'll leave everything to you. Handle it any way you think is best. Something light to start. And something simple to follow. We'll finish with a sweet touch, then fresh fruit if you have it." I nodded. The other two seemed perfectly content to let him order for them. "That's fine, Samuel. I'm sure you'll pleasantly surprise us. And bring us some wine. Something white for now, very good and very cold."

I nodded again. He smiled, and the girl looked up, and I suppose she smiled too. Except our eyes happened to catch and hold. She could have been naked from the neck down and just that once, looking into those fine, large eyes, I might not have noticed.

It wasn't until I was almost to the kitchen that I got my mind back on business. What struck me then was the way the young one had ordered. Most customers who came into the Fleur de Lis didn't trust themselves with a menu, let alone a waiter with carte blanche. Whether it was Howard's manner or the obvious interest of the girl, I don't know. But suddenly I had the urge to excel. It was a good feeling.

It was only when I thought about it later that I realized I hadn't been given a carte blanche at all. I'd been given freedom within limits that had been very carefully defined and, in Howard's case, well thought out beforehand. If I'd realized then it was to be the pattern of things, I'd have handed myself over to the police and saved everyone some time.

When I went into the kitchen, the chef had four orders working. He was a shapeless little guy with nothing but lines in his face and a hangdog expression that came mostly from Parakis giving him constant grief. When he looked up, he winced, out of habit I think.

"Listen, Umberto. I have three important clients. They want us to prepare something *bene*, eh? I told them the chef could work miracles."

He liked the "us," but I could see he didn't know whether to believe me or not.

Chefs are all the same: hangovers, brittle nerves, and sweat in the soup. But they're infants at heart. All a chef really cares about is food. To make one happy, you only have to let them know how much they're needed.

"Something *tutti ottimo*, Umberto." And I gave him a pleading look, sort of a Marcello telling Sophia that he really did care. Umberto shrugged, but I could see him starting to think. "Put it this way," I said, leaning forward. "What would you eat?"

He studied me a moment, then looked around the kitchen, all the time working with the other orders in a nice easy way that gave me just the slightest twinge of envy. He was a modest talent but a natural, which was more than I'd ever been able to boast. "Prawns," he said finally. "Fresh in the Boqué Risette. And the veal is nice."

I had him.

We worked out the rest of the order, Umberto as close to being happy as he ever would be in that kitchen.

I'd already decided on the flourishes. I wheeled out the trolley with all the hardware for flaming desserts on it. Flaming dishes is a bit of a con, but it's an impressive touch. It looks fancy, but all it takes is the right gestures and alcohol at the proper temperature. I seldom had any trouble at all.

When I had the trolley set up, I dug out a nicely chilled bottle labeled "Valmur," picked up an ice bucket, and scooted back to the garret.

The two men were talking with their heads close together. Howard doodled on a scrap of paper while the stump began working his way through a fresh cigar. Neil had brought some Cuban corona majors and socked him plenty for them. The stump didn't treat them as any luxury.

I wiped the bottle and flashed it around. No one appeared to care about the pedigree. I got rid of the cork and poured a drip into Howard's glass. An aroma wafted upward closer Rioja than Chablis. I held my breath while he lifted the glass to the light, swirled it, then tasted it.

He looked up with a slim smile. "Very nice wine, Samuel. Very nice indeed."

When I served the Boqué Risette, the girl said *ummm* and gave me a smile as though she were thinking about something other than food. With it they ordered another bottle of wine.

I hovered around the edge of things, just attentive enough to keep the wineglasses at a respectable level. There's a fine line between encouragement and an outright hustle. It didn't matter.

Whatever they were discussing had the men's attention completely. To most people waiters are like wallpaper, and it's surprising what you sometimes overhear. But above the noise of the restaurant and Piaf quivering through Jacques Charles' lyrics I could only catch bits and pieces.

I did find out the stump was named Caleb and the girl Davina. I was disappointed for no rational reason to find out they had arrived, together, the day before from the

States. Apparently the men were involved in a real estate transaction. I heard the Spanish word *villa* used several times, but I missed in what connection.

The girl seemed unconcerned, but obviously completely at ease in their presence. She ate silently, lost in her own thoughts. Once I looked up to find her watching me with an odd, questioning look I couldn't read. She smiled quickly, a broad, full-lipped smile, and let her eyes drop shyly as though embarrassed I'd caught her peeking. I don't know why their all looking so cozy together should have irritated me.

I might have understood her out on the town with Howard. But the one called Caleb looked uncouth enough to have been dropping ashes in his wine and talking as Americans often do, at fifty decibels when ten would do. Germans are just as bad.

In fact, Caleb wasn't talking much at all, except to ask an occasional question in a low tone I couldn't make out. Once or twice he stared at me blankly while he listened.

Toward the end of the second bottle of wine the conversation livened up. A little of the tightness went out of Howard's gestures and Caleb laughed a throaty gurgle every so often, grinning at me idiotically.

When I picked up the entree, Neil tried to catch my attention. I ignored him. I knew what he had on his mind. I wasn't sure I wanted to try a number on these people, even if I got the chance. I was in line for a good toke the honest way. I had no evidence that they had been made the least bit less attentive by what they'd had to drink.

The entree was a sizzling escalope orléanaise with dainty new potatoes and endives. I served it with some fresh cepe mushrooms sautéed in garlic and butter and tossed up a leaf salad with oil and lemon and put it in the center of the table.

I flourished a slope-shouldered bottle around with a label that advertised itself as a good second growth, St.-Julien. I went through the ritual again which nobody paid attention to and poured the wine. I caught the pungent smell of pure Algerian, cursed Parakis, and hoped that Caleb's cigar had deadened the rest of the noses around the table.

When Howard spoke, I nearly jumped a foot.

"Samuel, so far you've exceeded our expectations." His pale eyes seemed almost detached, absorbing what they saw like a pair of sponges. His voice was thicker.

"I try to do my best."

"You sure do, boy," said Caleb loudly. "You ought to sit right down here and have a glass of wine with us."

That was more in character. The wine was beginning to do the job after all. I declined the offer demurely, smiled my best enigmatic smile at Davina, who wasn't smiling for once, and exited.

Even before they finished the entree, I had the trolley in place.

I lit off the gas burner under the iron grill. The surest way to flop on your face with a crepe is to try it before the grill is just short of glowing and to use batter as thick as the way Umberto made it. It might have done for Aunt Jemima, not for a crepe.

In the kitchen I'd dosed the batter with milk and a double shot of cold water. The dark brandy and Grand Marnier were both close enough to the burner to warm nicely. If the crepe didn't go up like an erupting volcano, I'd turn in my badge.

At the exact moment the table was cleared, along with a second dead bottle of the St.-Julien, I served each of them an exquisite crepe suzette, glowing soft blue. The flame flickered out on cue. I left them to admire it in private. At times like that I began to think I did have the knack. But after all, it was only a crepe.

I brought back fresh fruit, some snifters, and a bottle of Remy Martin V.S.O.P. which I'd sniffed to make sure Parakis hadn't slipped in the Metaxa.

"With my compliments," I said.

Howard nodded jerkily. "That's generous, Samuel." It was nothing of the kind, of course. It was a rewarding tactic one way or another.

"Hey, boy," said Caleb, eyeing the bottle. He poked the end of a fresh cigar, rather unskillfully.

They sipped the brandy in silence. Howard tried awkwardly to peel a pear and gave up. Once Davina's eyes started to droop but snapped open again. Between the alcohol they had consumed and the jet lag they all appeared close to numbness.

Howard finally spoke with some effort. "Very nice, Samuel. Had enough, Caleb?" Caleb grinned stupidly. "The bill, Samuel. Bring the bill."

Which I did, after double checking it was correct. It came to a little over eighteen pounds. Howard glanced at it, nodded, and handed me a hundred-dollar bill. "Can you change this? Haven't had time."

"Of course."

He peeled off another from a roll that didn't seem any thinner with the two bills gone. "This too?"

I nodded.

Parakis snapped the bills, rubbed them, held them up to the light, and finally exchanged them at five percent above the bank rate. I frowned at him, but he shrugged and handed me the change. Three brown ten-pound notes, five fives, seven ones, and some silver.

Neil slithered up beside me. "Give 'em the rocket, Sammy."

"I don't know, Neil. Something doesn't feel right."

"They're stoned," he hissed. "I just looked."

I started to argue when he pulled me closer. "You owe me money, Samuel. You peel off some of that handful of paper in your hand or you'll be serving nothing but empty tables as long as you work here. It won't be all that long, I guarantee."

Parakis was watching us, one of his dark eyes beginning to wrinkle up like a prune. "Okay, Neil. But you know what?"

"What?" he said, grinning maliciously.

"You're a bloody shit-heel." I slipped one of the tens into my pocket and went back to the garret.

When I walked in, they were arguing halfheartedly

over changing hotels. Without interrupting I leaned forward and dealt the bills out at just the right speed, double counting one of the tens. I did it flawlessly, even better than I'd done the crepe.

Except the conversation stopped. I looked up to find Caleb, cigar poised in midair, a pink tip of tongue twisted in his lips. His eyes slid lazily from the bills to my face.

Howard's head swiveled slowly around. He looked at me out of the sides of his eyes.

Davina's surprise turned sad, and she looked away.

That's when I sensed I was in trouble. Not only had they seen my stunt. They had all seen it. Even Davina. Something began to bore a hole in my stomach about two inches beneath my navel.

I could have done one thing right then. Picked up the money and recounted it quickly, then exclaimed with surprise that the cashier had made a mistake, a very grave mistake.

Howard put his hand over the money.

"Boy, you surprise me," Caleb said quietly. There wasn't a trace of booziness in his voice. I had the oddest sensation he wasn't surprised at all.

Howard slid the money off the table and put it into his pocket without counting it. He moved around in his chair and looked at me carefully, his eyes narrowed in thought.

"Until now, Samuel, your performance has been impeccable, despite serving us Marqués de Riscal with a French label. You have imagination and style. That's important. You are obviously a professional, and Caleb and I appreciate watching a professional at work." He stood up quickly and put his face close to mine, the rest of it coming out between his teeth. "But you should stay in your own profession. In the other you are strictly an amateur."

"Howard . . ." Davina started to say. He cut her off with a sharp glance.

I stood there, mouth closed for once, braced for whatever was coming.

"Well?" said Caleb, looking at Howard, then back at me. He pulled in a long drag and waited about an hour before he let it out, his soft puppy-dog eyes on me. There was just the slightest amusement behind them.

I had the feeling he'd tossed the decision about my future to Howard, and Howard wasn't sure whether he wanted it. "I don't know," he said, flopping into a chair, his eyes trying to look inside my head again. "I just don't know."

"It's up to you, Howard."

Howard looked quickly at Caleb, then back at me. Then he made up his mind. He took the piece of paper he'd been doodling on, turned it over and scribbled something on it, and shoved it toward me.

"I want you at this address at ten tomorrow morning. Sharp, you get that?"

I said I had it. I'd have said anything at that moment to get those three out of there without making a stink.

Caleb chewed his cigar and said, "I bet that mean-looking pair of eyebrows behind the cash register wouldn't take kindly to the idea that you tried to cheat us."

Those puppy-dog eyes hid a lot of shrewdness. "No, he wouldn't," I said.

"Then you show up, boy." Howard was already moving toward the door. Caleb pulled out Davina's chair. She brushed past me, her eyes avoiding mine. Then they were gone.

Some brandy was left in the bottom of the girl's snifter. I downed it, catching the sweet nutty taste of her lipstick on the rim of the glass.

4

Of course I didn't plan on showing up the next morning or any other morning.

When I left the Fleur de Lis, I'd gone straight to a tatty little club on Westbourne Grove and drunk more brandies than I could count. I still didn't sleep worth a damn, the whole evening running over in my mind like a continuous newsreel.

What I couldn't understand was why Howard and Caleb hadn't done one of the following: Punched me in the nose and wrecked the place on the spot. Told Parakis I was a thief and counted out their change to prove it. Or been gentlemanly, given me a chance to humbly apologize, and forgotten about the whole thing. Instead, they'd let me keep the ten and invited me to meet them the next day, which no gambler I knew would have offered any odds on at all.

The only thing I could guess was they were after something, and it wasn't money. I'd already thought through the variations of the badger game, simple robbery and kidnapping. The idea of putting the grab on a waiter from the Fleur de Lis I couldn't have sold to Disney as an idea for a cartoon.

Whatever they wanted from me I had no interest in knowing. Howard's speech about professionals admiring professionals was firmly stuck in my mind. Whatever their profession was, it had nothing to do with mine. The way they had very carefully strung me out, then lowered the boom showed a calculation out of my league.

What they would do when I didn't show up at the address Howard had given me was another question. One call to Parakis with the details of what had happened the night before would end my short career as a waiter. Parakis would believe anything about his fellowman as long as it was bad. In my case it was not only bad but true.

I rolled around, trying to coax myself back to sleep, until the aroma of those mealy sausages the Brits eat for breakfast began creeping through the crack under the door. The rooming house I'd been forced to move into to feed my card habit already smelled of Lysol and old underwear. It was enough to turn a stomach stronger than mine.

I got up, brushed my teeth, stared at my puffy face in the mirror over the washbasin, and shaved it, going easy around the scar the Morgan had put on my chin.

When I finished shaving, I stuck a piece of Kleenex on a nick close to the scar, dressed, and rummaged through the flotsam on the top of the dresser. Two crumpled one-pound notes, eighty-five pence in silver, a stack of coppers, my Dupont lighter, a bent filter cigarette, a cellophane cigar wrapper, three soiled handkerchiefs —one with someone else's initial monogrammed on it— several cinema ticket stubs, a matchbook from a disco named the White Rabbit (a phone number scrawled in eyebrow pencil on the inside), and the note Howard had given me the night before. And lint. Lots of lint.

I looked at the note again. On one side was the name and address of a small expensive hotel in South Kensington, near Harrods. On the other side was the single word "Borrasa," traced over repeatedly as though someone had done it while thinking about something else.

I didn't want to know anything more about Borrasa or the three of them I kept telling myself. Except my thoughts kept coming back to the girl. I had the feeling she had been separate from their whole crass play, and more than mildly interested in Sammy Begay to boot. I hesitated about one second, put her out of my mind, and tossed the note in the wastebasket.

I called the Fleur de Lis from the pay phone in the hall. If I was to be fired, it would be *in absentia*. When the charwoman answered, I told her to tell Parakis I was sick. I would call when I was well. It wasn't such an exaggeration. Then I got out of there.

I walked out into a fine spring morning that had arrived about two months behind schedule. Hyde Park was a ten-minute walk. Space and trees and acres of grass seemed like the right environment to have a serious talk with myself.

I crossed the street, walking briskly south, and had gone about ten steps when I heard a voice call behind me: "Hey, Samuel."

I turned around and saw the racing-green MG parked at the curb, its engine turning over smoothly. From behind the wheel Davina gave me a sunny smile that went with the spring morning. She let the car roll up even with me, still smiling.

It was a nice smile, with lots of full lip and white teeth. It stayed fixed a little too long for comfort, like the one I'd seen Nixon flash on TV.

Davina was wearing a bright-orange cable-knit sweater, the kind that makes small breasts look big and Davina's abundant chest seem positively indecent. An expensive midi-length tweed skirt was hiked up her thighs to give her driving room. Her legs were brown and surprisingly well muscled.

"Good morning, madam," I said, with a cool Brit formality that generally keeps people at a polite distance.

"Quit kidding. It's 'miss' and you know it. Miss Williamson if you want to pretend, Davina if you don't." Her voice had the same kind of drawly accent as Caleb's, only without the rough edges, a coincidence I doubted.

"I'll pretend I walked out and you weren't here."

Some of the sunniness went out of her smile. "Don't be nasty, Samuel. I was out for a morning drive. I saw you cross the street." She watched me for a minute, then burst into a sharp laugh. "You don't believe me, do you?"

"Coincidences and miracles, Miss Williamson."

"What do you mean?"

"They may happen, but not to me. How long have you been waiting?"

Davina looked at me in a more interested way. "You shoot it pretty straight, don't you?"

"To everyone but myself, lady."

"All right," she said, a little defiantly. "I *was* waiting for you. I went to the restaurant and bribed the pretty thing with the hairdo to tell me where you lived."

"What did it cost you?"

"It doesn't matter. I wanted to apologize for the way Howard and Uncle Caleb treated you last night."

I took a close look at Davina and couldn't detect any sarcasm. When you look square into someone's face, you start at the mouth or nose. With Davina it was the eyes. Large and pale green and always moving, and whatever was happening on the rest of her face, they stayed permanently wary. At the corners were the hint of tiny wrinkles.

In bright sunlight Davina wasn't quite the young flower she had seemed in the soft lighting of the Fleur de Lis. But she wasn't any less stunning. Taut, classy features and fine skin, her face kept from the kind of perfect vacant beauty staring at you out of fashion magazines by that wariness around the eyes. They'd seen a lot and hadn't enjoyed much of it.

"I'm an honest twenty-seven, if that's what you're wondering." The tiny wrinkles deepened with the grin.

"I was wondering more why they suckered me last night."

"I don't know what you're talking about." Her gaze slid a few degrees off from mine and stared into space over my left shoulder.

"Your friends pretended all that booze put them in a stupor. Howard hadn't needed to change all that cash. Caleb paid for his cigars out of a fat roll of blues and browns. No one is going to get taken by the exchange rates in a restaurant unless they have a good reason. It was all cheese to tempt king rat."

She gave me a slow, exasperated nod. "You sure took long enough to figure it out."

"And a lot of brandy."

The exasperation turned angry. "You should have seen what they were doing right off. Boy, were you slow." It took me a minute to realize she was angry with *me*.

"Why did they do it?"

"Ask Howard. I'm not saying another word."

She reached over and opened the door on the passenger's side. "Come on. Get in." When I didn't move, she sat up and tilted her head. "Now you wouldn't be thinking of ignoring Howard's invitation, would you?"

"Some pigeons in the park depend on me for breakfast. I don't want to let them down."

Davina's eyes tightened slightly. "Look, Samuel. I think you're an attractive guy, even with a piece of Kleenex stuck on your chin."

"It's one of those mornings." I picked off the Kleenex and wondered if it ever happened to Steve McQueen.

"But don't get any cuter. For your health's sake, I mean." She smiled again and patted the seat next to her. "Do yourself a favor and jump in this little car. Pretend we're old friends." Her voice lightened a little. "It might be nice."

"And if I don't?"

"You'll find my brother isn't as patient as I am."

"Howard is your brother?"

"That's right, Samuel. And it wouldn't do to get him angry. He likes things to happen his way. When they don't. . . ." She hesitated and looked up. "I'm not supposed to tell you this, but it might be worth your time." She rubbed thumb and index finger together in the universal sign.

I'd been offered Davina's companionship and the hint of cash, one-two. When I still didn't jump, she added three, in the form of an undisguised threat. "It's me now, or Howard and Caleb later. You have to go home sometime, you know." Some of the hardness went from around her eyes. "Please, Sammy."

It was the tone in the "please, Sammy" that nailed it. "Some choice," I said, and climbed in. She pulled out sharply before I had a chance to change my mind, worked through a gear change smoothly, and made a dogleg left at the top of Queensway.

When we came to the Royal Lancaster Hotel, she made a tight turn on Barrow Street and cut south across Hyde Park. When we looped around the west end of the Serpentine, I caught her watching me out of the corner of her eye.

"Jesus, you are pale," she said, with a concern that seemed genuine. "That scar on your chin. Who clobbered you?"

"A car named Morgan. Suppose we talk about you people."

"You were supposed to be listening. Howard's my brother. The one that sounds like a hick is Uncle Caleb. The last name is Williamson."

"One big happy family."

"And it's best not to forget it," she said, her voice prickling sharply. "I trust them, and with men that's no small thing."

Davina's mouth looked suddenly as though she were biting a bullet. Our conversation had reminded her of something she preferred to forget.

Out of the corner of my eye I saw Davina glance at her watch and speed up sharply, wheeling the MG beneath Bowater House and into the top of Sloane Street.

The calculation of it started alarm bells clanging. Despite Davina's surprising concern for old Sammy's battered face, one female Williamson was doing a very skillful job of dropping me smack in the lap of Howard and Caleb, and behind locked hotel doors anything might happen.

Another thing I'd decided was that her remark about my having to go home sometime wasn't necessarily true.

What I'd left behind wasn't worth worrying about. It wasn't much of a home anyway.

When the joyride stopped, I made up my mind to step from the car lightly and if need be stride off in the direction of the nearest bobby and plead coercion and duress. That, after all, is what policemen are for.

I let my hand rest easily on the door handle.

Davina made a right-hand turn into Hans Crescent, found a parking spot, and slid the MG neatly between a maroon Bentley and a Daimler limo. A uniformed chauffeur sat in the Bentley sopping up anti-Establishment goodies from the *News of the World*, while Madam no doubt spent the day's dividends in Harrods.

In one motion she reached over and turned off the ignition and moved around toward me, bracketing my right arm with the soft mounds in her cable knit.

Her eyes were large and moist, and she looked on the verge of doing something very feminine.

"Listen, Sammy," she said, in a throaty way I don't hear "Sammy" said very often. "You're a brighter guy than I expected. And nicer, too. But next to Howard and Caleb you're nothing but a pussycat. Don't forget it." She pressed against me, and I could feel her breath quicken. "Be careful, will you?"

There was a suspended minute when neither of us said anything, me aware only of her body against my arm.

Before I could say anything to muck it up, she put a warm, moist hand on my cheek and kissed me softly, her lips leaving that same nutty sweetness in my mouth.

It put me right back to square one at pegging Davina.

Then she got out of the car without saying anything and walked toward the hotel not looking back, her slender hips and buttocks making tiny bounces beneath her tweed skirt.

I followed along, naturally. It seemed like the only thing to do.

5

I followed Davina through the door of Room 309 and caught the strong smell of good Cuban tobacco.

Howard and Caleb were there all right, hunched over a table in the middle of the room, giving it a very close inspection.

Howard stood bolt upright when he saw us, the only surprised expression I'd seen on his face before or since. Caleb's eyes went sideways, and the ash dropped off his cigar. From the look of it we'd caught them smoking behind the barn, if people still do that sort of thing.

"You're early, Davina."

"I'm sorry, Howard. I didn't realize—"

He cut her short. "No matter. It's nice to see you again, Samuel." His mouth twitched a half-smile at me. He made no move from the table.

Casually, Caleb lifted a sheet of paper about a yard square from the tabletop, let it hang by his thumb and forefinger, and brushed cigar ashes from it.

Poised that way, backlit by bright sunlight shining through one of the windows, I could see what was on it in a general sort of way.

It was a map of some kind, an island shaped roughly like a teardrop, full at one end and tapering narrowly at the other. Along one margin was a strip of what must have been coastline. That's all I saw before Caleb rolled it up quickly and handed it to Howard.

"If you'll excuse me for a moment, Samuel." He nodded curtly to Davina. She followed him into another room, and the door shut behind them.

Caleb stared at me a moment, his tongue making a lump in his cheek. "Drink, boy?"

I shook my head. "I haven't eaten yet."

"Never eat on an empty stomach if you can help it." He walked to the dresser, splashed two large shots of whiskey into water glasses from a bottle of Wild Turkey, and thrust one of the glasses toward me. I took it, just to be polite.

He eyed me over the rim of his glass. "I don't suppose you learned any new tricks since last night?"

"Very funny."

"Haven't seen a stunt like that since the Harlan County Fair in maybe '61 or '62. I figured double counting went out with the Stanley Steamer."

"Everything's up to date in Kansas City."

"You got an odd way of talking. What kinda name is Begay, anyway?"

"French. It was originally Begué." I spelled it for him. "My father Anglicized it when he became an American citizen. My mother's idea." It was a nice conversation and even better whiskey, but it was all a stall, and I wondered why.

If Howard was angry with Davina for bringing me in while the map was still on the table, he was being very quiet about it.

"How about cards?" Caleb said, still trying. "You any good at cards?"

If I'd said yes, it would have been a lie. He wasn't paying attention anyway. A pack of cards had already come out of his breast pocket, and his hands had undergone a miraculous transformation. His fingers were as stumpy as the rest of him, but wrapped around a deck of cards, they became nimble, his movements pure grace.

He worked the deck with one hand and did a couple of clean double cuts. Then he pushed the cards flat on the table and made a half dozen quick dealer's shuffles without the deck appearing to move at all. Next to his talent, my double counting a bill must have looked like a chimp in boxing gloves trying to peel a banana.

"Now you know," he said. I nodded. "Here, boy, I'll cut you for who mixes the next drink."

"It's eleven in the morning."

"I got a late start. Cut 'em."

The door to the other room opened when Caleb and I were on whiskey number three. Howard came through it briskly, his eyes darting between Caleb and me lolling around with our drinks.

By then I was beginning to relax. There had been a nervous moment following Davina out of the elevator when I thought maybe I was in for something nasty. After the first two minutes in the hotel room I guessed I wasn't going to be punched in the face or even threatened. I was the guest of honor. Except for that bloody map, things were developing about the way I expected.

"Let's get to business," Howard said stiffly. Davina closed the door to the other room behind her and padded silently off to an overstuffed moss-green chair in one corner, not looking so cheerful.

She glanced at me and turned her face away, rolling her eyes when I grinned back. She curled her long legs up under her and began filing her nails.

Howard said, "So you realize we played a little game with you last night?"

"That's right."

"And didn't you wonder why?"

"I did, but I didn't come up with any answers." Which wasn't true. I just hadn't liked the answers I got.

"A little test, Samuel. Caleb's idea. We like to know the limits of the people we deal with. Frankly, I was a little surprised when you went for it."

"You shouldn't have been," I said. The whiskey was rolling comfortably around my stomach.

Howard's eyes took on a look of sly amusement. "Why do you say that?"

"You people knew the Fleur de Lis was a clip joint, and you didn't walk in last night by chance."

"Well, I do tell," said Caleb, mildly surprised.

"Good, Samuel. Exactly right. Then you know why we went to the Fleur de Lis?"

"To have a look at me."

"Hey, boy, that's thinking," said Caleb, his eyebrows raised. I couldn't tell if he was having me on or not.

Howard's gaze narrowed. "And did you find that out from Davina?"

I pointed at Caleb. "Try Maverick here."

"Go on," grunted Caleb.

"I didn't tell you my last name. And Davina didn't find out my address from Neil this morning. He hasn't been out of bed before noon in his life. Someone's been snooping."

"Fine, Samuel," Howard said with a nod of approval. "We were scouting you for a very good reason."

That's where I drew a blank. I couldn't think of any good reasons, and I told them so.

"A certain Mr. Pohl thought you might fit our requirements perfectly," Howard said. "His judgment was better than I would have expected."

"Pohl?" It figured. Pohl was a ferret-faced Dutchman, a wine salesman I knew with a nose designed for smelling through garbage. Pohl probably knew more gossip about what went on in the kitchens of Europe than anybody. He undoubtedly knew of my recent withdrawal from the kitchen. "Pohl couldn't have told you anything good."

"On the contrary. What he said about you I found fascinating."

"But I don't want to eat none of your cooking," said Caleb. He grinned at me.

"Caleb . . ." growled Davina from the corner.

"You're not telling me anything I don't already know." I shoved my glass toward Caleb. "Let's have another drink."

He splashed another shot in my glass, a larger one in his own, and stuck the glass back in my hand. Howard waited until I'd had a sip.

"Your talents will suit us admirably, if you're interested. You see, Samuel, we have a proposition for you."

* * *

I'd been waiting for it. I sipped at the whiskey. It was going down rather easily. "And what if I'm not interested?"

"No problem, boy," replied Caleb casually. "Just give back the tenner you light-fingered last night and we'll forget it."

"If you want money, the line forms at the rear," I said, and knew I'd made a mistake.

Caleb's manner turned stony. "Then we might take it out in skin."

"Don't take Caleb too seriously." Howard smiled. "You're free to leave if you're not interested, no strings attached. But I think it would be an opportunity missed, Samuel. I really do."

They both watched me carefully. In the corner Davina had stopped filing her nails.

"I can't think of any help I might be to you gentlemen." I said it cheerfully.

"You're too modest, Samuel," Howard said, the patience beginning to wear off. "We're about to embark on a business venture in, for us, unfamiliar territory. Pohl said you knew the Continent well. I want you as an adjutant. Handle baggage, arrange transportation, and so forth. We will occupy a large house for perhaps two weeks and will entertain guests. You would supervise the help and make sure we eat and drink well. You see, all matters within your competence but for us time-consuming, tedious details. Pohl also said you spoke several languages." It sounded almost an afterthought.

I nodded.

"French?"

"Yes."

"Spanish?"

"Sufficient."

"Any others?"

"Italian. Some German, a little Greek."

"But the French is fluent?"

"I grew up in France. *La bêtise n'est pas mon fort.*"

Howard smiled thinly. "No, I'm sure stupidity isn't your strong suit. Nor was it Paul Valéry's. I think the words are his, are they not?"

"I don't know. It was something my uncle used to say."

Howard smiled at me. "You'll do just fine. I was sincere when I complimented you on your style last night, Samuel. You handle yourself with authority."

I didn't see what that had to do with anything. "And that's all?" I said. "Make sure you get to your destination, then run things while you're attending to business."

"Exactly right," said Howard, smiling quickly.

It sounded just fine, except I didn't believe a word of it.

"And the business is?"

Howard's smile slipped away. "No concern of yours."

"If it's crooked, forget it."

"I don't blame you, son." Caleb nodded sympathetically.

Howard began to look irritated.

"Samuel, in these times a border scarcely exists between honesty and dishonesty. In view of your performance last night, I find your remark surprising."

"It was a very small hustle," I said, "with me the only person likely to get bruised."

"You're absolutely right. Magnitude matters a great deal." His gaze wandered away for an instant before it snapped back. "Our enterprise is not, I admit, entirely lawful. As I explained, you will be nothing but an adjutant. I have no intention of letting you risk anything for which you are unprepared."

It sounded like very fine wording to me. Howard could have as much small print in the contract as he liked. I had already decided I'd agree to any bloody thing they wanted and walk out of the room intact and upright.

Howard was still talking. "It's not too difficult a task is it, Samuel, for fifteen hundred dollars?"

"Fifteen hundred dollars!" I cleared my throat. "That's seven hundred fifty a week."

"We better snap him up, Howard," Caleb said. "He's smart as a whip."

Davina stared a dagger at Caleb, who put a hand quickly over his mouth and made a what-did-I-say? face.

Howard leaned across the table, looking straight at me. "That's right, Samuel, fifteen hundred dollars."

There was a long silence in the room, and I had a feeling they expected me to swallow it right there. When I didn't, Howard coughed uncomfortably. For once, I hadn't done exactly what they thought I'd do.

Howard reacted quickly. "Now don't rush into things, Samuel. Take the rest of the day to think it over. If you want the job, it's yours. Simply meet us at Charing Cross Station at precisely four o'clock this afternoon. We have a train to catch at four thirty sharp. If you're not there"—he shrugged a little too casually—"we'll know you're not coming and make other arrangements. That's fair enough, isn't it?"

Any guy who could phrase questions like that would never go hungry in this world. Or worry about a pair of silky thighs to crawl between. I said yes because there was really no reason to say no.

Howard grinned with what might have been a large dose of smug satisfaction. "Good, Samuel, good." He took my arm and piloted me toward the door in one smooth maneuver. "Now if you think of any questions, anything at all, you call me. I'll be here all day."

At the door he patted me on the shoulder and fixed me with a sincere gaze that came on like a spotlight. "Come with us, Samuel, and I promise you you'll return a healthier, wealthier man." He pulled a fat roll of bills from his pocket and peeled off a ten-pound note. "Have lunch on me and think about that. I know you'll make the right decision."

"I'm sure I will, Mr. Williamson."

"Howard is the name, Samuel." He poked the bill into my breast pocket and winked at me. "There's more where this came from, remember that."

"I'll remember."

Before the door closed, I caught a glimpse of Davina. She was holding her left hand out at arm's length, concentrating on her handiwork with the nail file.

I was still watching her when the door clicked quietly shut behind me.

6

A half block from the hotel was a Kentucky Pancake House, done up in red plastic and neon. It would have looked right on Forty-second Street, but stuck in among stately Edwardian, it was a wart on an attractive lady. A sign in the window said "Fresh pizza served." I went in anyway, ordered breakfast, and, while I waited, phoned British Rail.

Howard had mentioned meeting them at Charing Cross Station. I found out the only train leaving Charing Cross at four thirty that afternoon was an express to Southampton. Along with being the largest port in southern England, Southampton was also the terminal for the Swedish-Lloyd ferry to Spain.

The idea that the Williamson business venture might happen in Spain fitted the name Borrasa on the slip of paper and the bits of conversation I'd overheard at the Fleur de Lis the night before. It also fitted Howard's question about how well I spoke Spanish, although I'd had the impression he was more interested in my French.

What didn't fit anything so far was the map. They hadn't wanted me to see it, and they hadn't said a word about it.

Neither Howard nor Caleb had seemed as willing to chew me up and spit out the bones as they had the night before. The truth was I had a hunch Howard wasn't so cocksure of himself after all. His delivery had been a little too forceful, as though if he didn't hard-sell his confidence, you might begin to question him. I don't think he wanted that.

More than once I'd had the feeling Caleb knew

Howard was overplaying it, the way his eyes had wandered away. Yet he'd let Howard go on, as if for some reason it were important to let Howard discover his own mistakes.

Despite myself, I had a growing, grudging respect for old Caleb. Underneath that sleepy manner was a genuine self-confidence you don't get for nothing. Somewhere, sometime, Caleb had laid himself on the line, found out exactly who he was, and decided he measured up pretty well.

Davina was the puzzle. Sitting there, those fine legs wrapped around like spaghetti, she'd made a point of ignoring me. Either the moist-eyed body rub in the car had been designed for the sole purpose of luring me to the hotel room, willingly, or she felt she'd let me see a soft side of her she wasn't particularly proud of, and she was making up for it. I remembered her remark about not trusting men and that wary look in her eyes.

Lovely Davina's troubles I didn't need. If I could have forgotten her fragrances and the way she felt when she leaned against me, it would have been easier. Less gonads, more brains, Begay.

One thing was sure. They didn't need to pay fifteen hundred dollars for what Howard said he wanted me to do. He could have found servants in Barcelona or Madrid who would forget their names for half that. Howard had it in his head I was essential to them.

Whatever they were up to, the atmosphere in the hotel room had been charged enough to make me sure it was something big.

And with the name Borrasa and the glimpse I had of the map I knew more about their scheme than they thought I knew. It had the distinct smell of money.

At that point Manning Able's reasoning voice crept in, calmly reminding me what a bloody, self-deceptive fool almost anyone can be, under the right set of circumstances.

That's the trouble with a shrink. There's never a simple reason for things, because who would pay to hear something they could come up with themselves? I was obviously preoccupied with money because I'd been weaned early or put on the potty late. It would never have been anything as straightforward as I needed the cash because I was stone broke. Who wanted an analyst's advice anyway? What I really could have used was another drink.

When my breakfast arrived, it was perfectly obvious Kentucky ought to stick to bourbon and horses. A couple of yellowed pebbles stared up at me, with some pitiful shreds of bacon on the side. I could have cooked it myself.

I paid my check, left a toke out of principle, and caught a cab to the British Museum. I practically owed it to myself to try to fill in the spaces.

Papa Victor would have been proud of me, anyway. When fortune knocks with a heavy hand, he used to tell me, it sometimes takes courage to answer.

Later I remembered another saying of his: Some people never learn when to quit winners.

The map room of the British Museum was on the second floor above the north entrance, next to a department of prints and drawings. By the time I found it it was nearly noon.

The assistant curator was a man named Merwin. He was a very old man to be an assistant anything. When I walked in, he was watching the second hand move around the big clock over the door, his eyes, I was sure, following it in a slow revolution.

"Now what exactly is it you want?" he said, sliding his eyes away from the clock almost reluctantly.

"I'm looking for an island."

"I see," he said, rather distastefully. "There are quite a number, you know."

I described the island I'd seen on the map, adding that it might be Spanish. Merwin made a small hum, and his face took on a more lively look.

"How big was it?" he asked, his eyes becoming positively intense. "The size of the map, I mean."

"About so-by-so." I showed him. He hummed again and led me briskly along a row of upright racks with wide drawers.

He slid open one of the drawers. The maps were all of islands. We went through the Balearics, but they were all the wrong shape. Then we went on to the Canaries. An island named La Palma looked the right shape except the teardrop was upside down.

Something wasn't right, but I couldn't have said what. I obviously didn't know so much after all. My earlier confidence had been nine-tenths whiskey on an empty stomach. The heavy breakfast had taken off the edge. I began to realize that the connection I had made between the Williamson business venture, the name Borrasa, and the island might only have been in my head. Then I remembered the thing I couldn't put my finger on. I told Merwin about the strip of coastline along one margin of the map.

He sighed, slid one drawer shut and another open. He whipped back a fabric cover to expose a stack of maps several inches thick. My stomach began stirring around in a good way for a change. The map on top was the same dimensions as the one I'd seen in Caleb's hands.

Merwin said, "It's obviously not an oceanic island at all. This is a Spanish ordinance series, the *Mapa Militar* they call it. It's scaled at 1:50,000, about a mile to the inch, and covers a good deal of the coastline. Naturally it catches a number of the litoral islands close by." He gave me a conspirator's grin. "Shall we have a look?"

We worked our way around the coast sheet by sheet. It took less than ten minutes to find it.

"Is that your island?" he asked. He was pleased with himself.

"Yes indeed," I said. In the top right-hand corner of the sheet was the name Tiburón.

Merwin looked at the island and gave his chin an appraising tug. "I can see it, I suppose."

"See what?"

"*Tiburón* is Spanish for shark. The island looks something like a shark, especially when you consider this." His bony finger traced the outline and stopped at a large crescent-shaped bay making a deep indentation in the widest part of the island. "It does look something like a shark's mouth, don't you think?" He gave me a gleeful smile. "Open, of course, as though it were ready to devour—"

"What are those little black squares around the bay?" I said, before Merwin's imagination dragged me in with it.

He bent closer. "Odd. I would have said it was a small village, except it has no name. Quite unusual for the Spanish. Hold on a minute." He scooted away and returned a moment later carrying a volume of Moore's *Encyclopaedia of Places*. "This might give us the answer." He fingered through it, found a page and went down it mumbling through Tibesti, Tibeszi, and two other Tiburóns. "Ah," said Merwin.

"What does it say?" By this time he had me hooked.

"Island in province of Almería, three miles east southeast of seaport La Boca. Private. Area twelve square miles, population (1960) forty-eight persons. Exports olive oil, wine, fruit. Once site of Moorish fort controlling access to the port of Almería." Merwin looked up. "Perhaps that's it."

I didn't answer him. I was thinking about the word "private."

Merwin dug out another smaller scale map of the entire region that gave a better perspective. The whole Golfo de Almería was a big bite out of the coast of southern Spain. The crescent-shaped bay on Tiburón faced away from the Spanish coast with nothing between it and the coast of Morocco except about one hundred miles of Mediterranean. Whatever else there was to know about Tiburón I wasn't going to get it from a map.

Merwin walked me out, humming contentedly to himself, and I had the impression my visit had made his day. At the door he gave me a cheerful wave.

"Enjoy yourself," he said brightly. "And don't drink the water."

It took me another hour to track down Al Vásquez. I found him in a blue-tiled Spanish bodega and cafe in Soho, sitting long-faced over a glass of fino. I had never known Al to have anything other than a long face, but he was in good company. All the people in there had sad expressions. Most of them were exiled for one reason or another from half the countries in Latin America, with Spain, Portugal, Angola, and Mozambique thrown in.

Al Vásquez worked as a waiter in a very elegant Spanish restaurant near Regent Street until the time Alonso Blas Vásquez de Prado could go back to Spain, walk over the grave of Franco, and assume the head of the royal household of Vásquez.

I sat down with him and ordered coffee. I talked about the tourists and the weather and Wimbledon and avoided Spanish politics. It wasn't easy. Al could usually twist anything you said around to the shafting the monarchy got from Franco. Any other time I might have listened. I finally asked him point blank if the name Borrasa meant anything to him.

Al didn't even blink. "If you mean Luis Borrasa, don't be silly."

"I just asked."

"Of course I know of him."

"Well known, is he?"

Al made an exasperated sigh. "Sammy, where have you been? Everyone has heard of Borrasa."

The anxious tickle began to creep into my stomach again.

"Because he's rich?"

Al waggled a finger at me in a Latin way that means no. My stomach stopped tickling. "Superrich. Like Getty or Onassis. One of the richest men in Spain. Mining, steel, ships, hotels, Borrasa is in them all. The press calls him the Lion."

"Why the Lion?"

"Because he devours everything he sees. He climbed his way to the top on the bodies of his friends, they say, and lived to enjoy his wealth and theirs. I suppose you'd call him ruthless. In my country the word means little. Besides, people like Borrasa have no consciences, only stomachs."

I felt the conversation beginning to make its inevitable turn. I bought Al another fino, had one myself, then asked him if he'd ever heard of an island named Tiburón.

"Sammy, what have we just been talking about?"

"Money."

"Luis Borrasa," he corrected.

"Right, right."

"Then you ought to know that much, at least."

"Know what?"

"Tiburón is the family home of the Borrasas."

Bingo.

7

I was at Charing Cross Station a few minutes early. The place had the din of a steel mill. The rush-hour crowd was beginning to well up, and it took me a minute or two to spot Howard.

He was waiting in the middle of the main concourse, dressed sharply in a dark suit. A trench coat was draped casually over one arm, but there were no bags in sight. No Davina or Caleb either, for which I was thankful. One Williamson was enough.

Howard grinned tightly when he saw me. "Glad you decided to join us. We took the liberty of picking up a few essentials from your room for you. Now come along."

"Hold on, Howard. I have questions, after all."

The grin didn't disappear but seemed to shrink tighter. "Now now. We've a train to catch."

He took my arm, but I didn't budge. "Not until I know where Borrasa fits into your business venture. And that island of his, Tiburón."

Howard turned around and faced me straight on then. He looked into my eyes and nodded. "Good, Samuel. I've been right about you all along. You're smart, and that pleases me."

"It pleases me, too, but I'm not getting any answers."

"In fact, I just won one hundred dollars from Caleb because you're so smart."

"What is that supposed to mean?"

"Caleb said you wouldn't put it together. I bet you would."

"Put what together?"

Howard laid a friendly hand on my shoulder. "Now, Samuel, you don't think you saw anything we didn't want you to see?" He looked genuinely surprised. "The name Borrasa wasn't on that slip of paper by accident. And Davina wasn't early today. Her arrival was precisely calculated, as was her moment of tenderness in the car, I assure you. I was afraid for a minute we'd been too subtle with the map. When you didn't bother to ask about it, I knew you'd seen it after all."

"You wanted me to find out about Borrasa?" I was shouting loudly at Howard, the sound of it absorbed in the cacophony around us.

"Calmly, Samuel," Howard said, giving my shoulder a soothing pat. "There is no better way to involve a person in something than to let him figure it out for himself. It stimulates the imagination, doesn't it?"

The fact that he was absolutely right made it sting all the more. He saw the look on my face and broke into satisfied laughter. I looked at Howard, anger beginning to rise.

"Besides," said Howard, prodding me almost jovially, "if I had told you our little venture involved the very rich Señor Borrasa and a trip to Spain, you would have disbelieved me or, worse, done something rash. In which case we might have had to bring you against your will. Not easy to do, I assure you. As it is, here you are."

I remembered when I was seven or eight years old living in Washington Heights, there had been a big bully of a kid, a Mexican strangely enough for that part of the world, named Rolly. Rolly and I used to fight regularly every Friday for reasons I can't remember, and another thing I can't remember is ever winning. I have a very clear picture of Rolly sitting on my chest taking my own fists and smacking me in the face with them over and over, laughing in the same self-satisfied way Howard was doing just then. I had just enough of the same feeling of frustration to make me remember that I didn't like getting my own efforts tossed back in my face. If I'd had any thoughts about joining the Williamson enterprise, I had just changed them.

"You went to a lot of trouble for nothing. Hire yourself another boy."

"I detect a certain irony in your voice, Samuel. You've no doubt guessed I have something more in mind for you."

"You offered me too much money," I said defiantly. "A bill a week and I would have been hanging on your coattail."

"I find that hard to picture, but a good point. I'll remember it in the future. Now come on."

"You didn't hear what I've been saying. No story, no Begay."

"At this moment out of the question. Sorry."

"Me too. I could have used the cash. I've changed my mind anyway. Now it's just no Begay."

Howard's eyes narrowed, surprised. "You're not coming?"

"That's what I mean."

His eyes stayed on me, and the surprised look was replaced by something else. It was time for an exit. I always did have a bad sense of timing. I started to turn, but Howard's friendly hand on my shoulder didn't shake off.

He caught me pivoting on the wrong foot and spun me back around off-balance, pulling me toward him in the same motion. No one passing nearby even batted an eye. The hand with the trench coat over it pressed against my stomach. This time there really was something boring into me just below the navel.

I looked down and saw the ugly glint of a thin steel blade. The knife must have been in his hand under the coat the entire time.

Oddly enough I had a brief sharp mental replay of the accident in the Morgan. Part of me was in it, involved and helpless, while another part was outside myself watching it all happen and recording calmly my reactions to the whole bloody calamity.

My only thought was how uncharacteristic a weapon. Howard should have had a gun in a shoulder holster. A knife, a long, thin stiletto, was so . . . Latin. I could feel the sharp point through my trousers.

"I'm afraid I don't have a choice," Howard said almost apologetically. "I hope you understand that."

"You're going to a lot of trouble to hire yourself a flunky."

"I'm afraid it's more critical than that."

"You wouldn't use that knife here," I heard myself say.

"Of course I would," he replied calmly. "I'd be a mile away before any of these good citizens would stop to ask you what was wrong. And you could look forward to eating gruel the rest of your life. That's if you lived, of course."

The thought was enough to convince me. I walked with him through the station. He gave two tickets to the conductor at the entrance to gate twenty-one. We walked the length of the train until we came to a car marked first class. Through a window Davina looked out at us.

"Don't say I didn't warn you," she said, when Howard slid shut the door to a first-class compartment. He flashed her an odd look but didn't say anything. A minute later Caleb arrived.

"Well, look who's here," he said happily.

"Better make yourself comfortable, Samuel," Howard said. "We have a long way to go together."

"Answer me a question, will you?"

Howard looked as though I were interrupting his thoughts.

"That depends on the question."

"What if I hadn't shown up?"

"It wouldn't have mattered. We'd already worked out scenarios for you, Samuel, and had taken them into account."

"That's his way of saying we guessed the probablies," Caleb said. "What you'd probably do. Then what you'd probably do if you didn't do that."

"And what if I'd done the smart thing and run as far and as fast as my little feet would take me?"

Caleb got a thoughtful look on his face and picked tenderly at the back of his neck. "Been riding around behind you all day asking myself the same question."

I looked into his open face and wondered if I'd ever know when he was bluffing and when he wasn't. "You made a good job of staying hidden."

"Hell, boy," he said, "you didn't even look."

8

Three days later we were nestled into a white stuccoed farmhouse two kilometers from the village of La Boca. From the patio I could look across three miles of azure Med at the hazy, blue-gray outline of Borrasa's island, Tiburón.

The ferry out of Southampton was a good-sized motorship named the *Saga*. I shared a cabin with Caleb, his cigars, and half a case of bourbon. Needless to say, Begay was not to have his privacy.

I felt bloody trapped. Papa Victor always said it was a big jump from a good amateur to even a so-so professional. I understood for the first time what he meant. I didn't know how good they were, but Howard and Caleb were pros. They'd suckered me, outthought me, and worked me around like a piece of putty.

"Happens to the best of us, boy," Caleb consoled. "The trick is not to let it keep happening."

"You'd have liked my Uncle Victor."

I finally agreed to play cribbage with him if he let me deal every hand, hoping I'd find out more about the Borrasa venture.

By the time we reached Bilbao thirty-six hours later I owed him eighty dollars and had a hangover that would have staggered a bull. "You got to concentrate, boy," said Caleb, giving me a shiny grin. He hadn't said a word about where we were headed or why.

A couple of other things happened between the ship and the farmhouse that convinced me Howard and Caleb were going to reveal nothing more than they had to.

We went through Spanish immigration and customs in a pack, me back to belly between Howard and Caleb. "Be very cool," Howard had warned me, choosing at that moment to clean his fingernails with that long, thin stiletto.

The *oficios* didn't pay any attention to me, anyway, which was the idea I suppose.

I think I got my first look at the real Davina right then. How she managed to lean so far toward the rooster in uniform checking passports without falling over I'll never know. Lips parted, that same wide-eyed look of vulnerability I'd seen in the MG before she'd planted a kiss on me and lured me into the hotel.

The rooster smiled a mouthful of gold teeth and let his beady black eyes rest squarely on Davina's creamy bosoms trying to crawl out the top of her scoop-necked blouse. He barely looked at the passports, stamping in the *entradas* like a machine. I had a look, though. I couldn't watch Davina's performance anyway, although I don't know why it should have bothered me. It was her life.

Both Caleb and Davina had new passports made out in their own names. Howard's was dog-eared, the blue fading to a dirty green. The picture in it was his, all right. Except the passport was made out in the name of Howard Jamison.

I didn't doubt Howard was a Williamson. He displayed too many of the devious characteristics I was beginning to realize ran through the whole clan. There were a dozen other reasons why Howard might want to enter Spain as someone other than Howard Williamson, all criminal.

Climbing into a taxi, Davina brushed against me, and I let it out before I had a chance to think. "That was some performance, Davina. I really enjoyed that."

She blinked at me, as if she honestly didn't know what I was talking about. Then she blushed. "Don't be stupid, Sammy. That was just business." She looked at me differently. "Besides, I didn't really think you cared."

In the taxi on the way to the railway station Howard held out his hand. "Passport and money, Samuel."

It was a little late to argue. I gave them to him. He handed the passport to Caleb, who stuffed it into a coat pocket.

The idea I supposed was to make me think twice before walking into the *retrete* and trying to climb out a window. The Spanish police are notably inhospitable to foreigners without money or documents. By the time I could have made them believe that a full-grown, healthy young man past the age of consent had been kidnapped for no reason he could explain, Howard's business venture would be wrapped up and the money in the bank.

At Bilbao we boarded a big RENFE diesel and by early evening were in Madrid. We changed trains and continued south. It wasn't until the next morning in Granada that I learned Howard was no longer with us.

I was standing on the station platform trying to blink the grit out of my eyes when Caleb handed me the note. "Time to earn your keep, boy."

"Do I have a choice?"

"No," he said, lighting up his first cigar of the day. I read the note.

It said: "Samuel. Hire inconspicuous car Granada. Take road south to Motril, then east to La Boca." There was a sketch map showing me where I was to go from there. "At farmhouse see Señora Muñoz. Stay put until I arrive." The last line was underlined. It was signed H.

My Spanish was rusty, but Caleb's money was good. At a garage near the station we rented a SEAT 850, which is nothing but a Spanish-built Fiat with a lot more rough edges left on it than an Italian would have been satisfied with.

Caleb observed it had been designed for jockeys but hefted his bulky frame into the back seat, handing me the keys.

I hadn't been behind the wheel of a car since I'd wrecked the Morgan, and I wasn't so sure Manning

Able's warning about staying out of automobiles was a joke.

"Whose idea was this?" I said to Caleb.

"Not mine, boy, you better believe that."

"Come on, you two," Davina said. She legged her way into the front seat with me and gave my hand on the gearshift a warm squeeze.

I nosed the SEAT into the traffic and followed everyone else's lead. Eyes straight ahead, glassy stare, foot on the gas, and lots of horn.

I found the Paseo Violón and followed it straight through the middle of Granada heading south.

By late afternoon we'd climbed over the Sierra and dropped down to the coast. By Motril we could have been in Africa. Oranges, date palms, and a polished whiteness to the villages that seemed all the brighter after London's gray fringes. For once I'd have swapped one for the other hands down.

It wasn't a part of Spain I had any feeling for at all. I'd spent two years with Papa Victor in Barcelona, which is almost another country. To hear the Catalans of the northeast tell it, the rest of Spain is dragged along on their coattails, and the people south of Tarragona are all goat herders or gypsies. The description didn't fit what I knew about Luis Borrasa.

I couldn't imagine what the Williamsons thought they could get away with. Even the poor in Spain build walls around themselves, because history has shown them that their neighbors are the ones to worry about. But the Spaniard will do the wall one better and line the top of it with broken bottles, because he not only wants to keep people out; he wants to be remembered as someone it doesn't pay to fool with. An eye for an eye is never quite good enough for a Spaniard. Two eyes for a toenail would be closer to it. With Borrasa's money he'd have more than a wall with a few broken bottles.

Whatever they were planning had better be good.

By the time we'd reached La Boca the humidity had dropped and the temperature gone up. The landscape looked as though it had been gouged and plucked clean, then scorched to make sure nothing with more shade than an olive tree would grow on it by chance.

The woman Howard mentioned in his note, Señora Muñoz, greeted us without a smile when I drove the SEAT along a dusty drive and into the courtyard of the farmhouse, following Howard's map.

She was about forty or so with raven-black hair pulled back in the classic style. She'd been beautiful once, and in her hard-faced way she still might have been considered attractive, from a comfortable distance.

While Caleb and Davina unpacked, I had a look around. When I walked into the kitchen, Señora Muñoz walked in behind me and stood there with her hands on her hips. A dark scowl, growing darker each second, said it clearly.

She was in command of the kitchen, the farmhouse, the whole damned place.

9

My only satisfaction during the next week came from the discovery that Señora Muñoz was just as growly with Caleb.

She forbade him to smoke his corona majors in the house in a blistering rattle of Andalusian Spanish that didn't need translation. She was a tough old crow. And it was apparent she was more than just hired help.

Behind the main farmhouse was a small house for the servants. But Señora Muñoz lived in the bedroom next to Davina's in one wing of the main house. Caleb and I were in another wing, rattling around in four bedrooms each big enough for an army. When I remarked we could have done with less space, Caleb squinted at me.

"Just you wait, boy," he said, and added a look that meant he'd doled out my week's supply of information and I wasn't getting any more.

Another thing happened I thought at first was due to Señora Muñoz's nagging. Caleb went off the bottle.

By the time I was out of bed the first morning Caleb was already in the kitchen, a towel around his neck, the sweat standing out on his forehead.

"Are you feeling all right?" I asked.

"Course I'm all right. Been out for a little roadwork." He danced around, feinted a couple of lefts, and cackled to himself. I didn't see him take a drink again. In a couple of days the loose skin around Caleb's jaw began to tighten, and his moves took on a little of the quickness of Howard's.

I barely saw Davina. After morning coffee she would

pad off to her bedroom, doing I knew not what until dinner. Caleb spent the better part of each day in the servants' quarters. The door he made a point of keeping tightly shut had a shiny new lock. Both Davina and Caleb seemed absorbed in their preparations with an intensity that only made me feel more uneasy. On the rare occasions I saw Davina out of her room she'd give me a distant smile and disappear again before I could get close enough to make polite conversation.

All in all, I was suddenly ignored. The third day I decided to find out how much.

The farmhouse was set on twenty acres or so of untended olive trees, without another house in sight. The keys to the SEAT were in Caleb's pocket, but I knew the general direction of La Boca. After lunch I waited until Caleb had gone into the servants' quarters and Señora Muñoz was busy gutting a chicken, handling a knife very skillfully I noted, before I wandered off on a stroll.

A couple of hundred yards into the olive groves I eased a look around. Caleb was about fifty feet behind me studying bird life in the olive trees. He gave me a surprised grin, as though he had just that second seen me. But later that night he stared at me across the dinner table without smiling.

"It wouldn't do to get too restless, boy."

But I was more than restless. If it weren't for the atmosphere of impending calamity, it would have been a holiday. Color was back in my face. I hadn't had a drink of hard liquor in days. I was clearheaded in the morning. I was also as randy as a barnyard rooster, which might have been part of the reason Davina gave me such a wide berth. If she'd ruffled my feathers, I'd have jumped and flown around the room. By the end of a week my nerves were strung taut. At least Caleb and Davina, and probably Señora Muñoz, had one advantage. They knew what came after the waiting.

If I couldn't walk away from the farm, I made up my mind to find out what came next.

I didn't get a chance until the seventh morning, when Caleb broke the routine.

After coffee Davina disappeared into her room. As usual Caleb went straight to the servants' quarters. Ten minutes later he came out again, climbed into the SEAT, and drove off, without a word to anyone.

I didn't think it likely Caleb would be gone long enough for me to cover the distance to La Boca. I wandered around until I determined Señora Muñoz was involved with housework. Then I went straight to the servants' quarters. Whatever Caleb found so interesting inside had to have a bearing on their intentions with Luis Borrasa.

I didn't even bother with the front door, but went around to the back. I found the back door bolted from the inside.

I ended up jimmying a kitchen window and sliding through into a kitchen that would have rented as a self-contained flat in London for twenty-five quid a week. If that was how the poor lived, it made you wonder about progress.

Through an arch was a sitting room about fifteen feet square, with nothing in it but a longish wooden table and a dozen heavy oak chairs.

I pushed open the door to what must have been the bedroom and walked through it smack into the armory.

Along one wall was a new, roughly built workbench, with three powerful lights dangling from the ceiling above it. Lined up neatly against another wall were ten shiny new machine pistols. At the end of the row were three crates marked "British Service Ball 9mm Parabellum (115 gr.)" There were two larger-type machine guns on heavy four-legged mounts and several other crates broken open to reveal shiny brass bullets.

On the workbench were two well-oiled automatic pistols, some odds and ends of electrical equipment, several yards of nylon rope knotted every couple of feet. About a dozen skinny wax-paper-covered bricks, about a foot long, that stank to heaven were laid across wooden slats so air could circulate beneath them. I didn't know what they were until I picked up a dog-eared book titled Dupont's *Blasters Hand-book*; then I made a guess. There was also an eight-page rental agreement for the farmhouse in Spanish, with me named as principal.

I'd seen enough to confirm that whatever was happening on Tiburón involved more than the Williamsons. And it was going to make a great deal of noise. Begay, I decided, had best not be around.

I should have made the decision a minute sooner. When I turned to leave, Caleb was standing in the doorway, chewing a dead cigar, watching me as though I were the proverbial fish in the barrel.

"You got bad habits, boy." He tamped the end of the cigar against the doorframe, then dropped it onto the floor and ground it slowly with his foot. "Why don't you relax and enjoy the sun, instead of getting all snoopy?"

"Because snooping is the only way I find anything out. No one is volunteering anything."

He let his eyes move over the items on the workbench. "So what have you found out?"

"That Howard's spent time in a Spanish jail." It was a wild shot, thrown from about as far back as I could reach. Caleb's face kept a studied sameness that I knew by now was his automatic reflex guaranteed to dampen any show of emotion.

"You didn't find that out snooping around here."

"I saw Howard's passport, with a name that wasn't his. If he'd served time here for something serious, he'd probably be *persona non grata* as Howard Williamson. Maybe he's still wanted."

"He ain't. Not that it makes a difference." Caleb squinted at me. "I got to watch you. You might be pretty smart, after all. What else you found out?"

"Nothing. Not a thing." I stared at Caleb hard. "Caleb, look around for chrissakes. This stuff isn't for a bird shoot. Something big is going to happen."

"I take back what I said. Of course something big is going to happen." He began to look at me a little funny. "Hell, boy."

"I want out."

"You're in. Sit back and enjoy it."

"I don't even know what the big *it* is."

"You'll find out when Howard feels like telling you."

"It's his idea?"

"Sure is, boy. You want to learn you got to play for money, never forget that." It was a remark I remembered later. "Howard has himself one fine plan." He tugged at his chin and raised one eyebrow. "I could show you that." The idea seemed to amuse him.

"All right, I'll look at the plan," I said quickly.

Caleb plucked at an earlobe, his mouth turning down. "Wouldn't do you no good, though. Doubt you'd understand it any better than I did."

"Probably not."

Caleb squinted at me again. "I don't know. You're learning fast. I shouldn't have mentioned the plan."

I didn't know if Caleb was getting his kicks from teasing the city slicker or what. "Caleb, I don't care what you and Borrasa end up doing to each other."

"Now don't get flustered. You don't see Davina all worried, do you?" I couldn't see the connection. "You'll find out what you need to know soon enough." He gave me a sleepy grin. "More than you want, maybe."

10

Caleb was right. I found out in a way and at a time I wasn't prepared for. Papa Victor used to say that you had to be careful what you wanted in this world, because you very often got it.

Since it had a better sound than most things he used to say, I expect he read it somewhere.

That night Señora Muñoz put together a magnificent dinner of chicken baked with langostinos, served with grainy saffron rice and a cold sharp-tasting white wine.

Caleb stared at the wine, sighed, and had mineral water. Davina had several glasses and began to lose a little of the glums that had been on her the entire week. I finished the bottle, ignoring the dark look Señora Muñoz put on me practically from the start of dinner.

It was late by the time we'd finished. The hour of the burro overcame us all, predictably. Caleb yawned, Davina yawned, Señora Muñoz scowled, and we went our ways to bed, separately as usual. I watched Davina walk away toward her wing of the house, her hips moving in interesting undulations.

I'd pushed the thought out of my mind enough to drop off to sleep when the phone downstairs began to ring for the first time since we arrived.

A few minutes later there were footsteps outside my door, and a loud click.

I'd been locked in.

When I heard the SEAT start in the courtyard, I climbed onto the bed and looked out.

The window was about two feet square, closer to the

ceiling than the floor, but I could see the courtyard clearly. A minute later Señora Muñoz came out of the farmhouse and crossed in front of the headlights, carrying a small wicker suitcase.

She climbed into the passenger seat, and the SEAT bounced off along the drive, Caleb at the wheel.

I didn't hesitate a moment. Caleb and Señora Muñoz weren't off on a joyride. I had the feeling the phone call had set something in motion that wouldn't stop until it ground Begay up in its machinery. I hopped off the bed, went to the door, and twisted the wrought-iron doorknob, but it wouldn't budge.

I dressed anyway, put on my shoes, and began wondering whether I could fit through the window and drop twelve feet to the ground without damaging anything vital. I was up on the bed again, hands on the window ledge ready to try, when the door latch clicked and the heavy oak door opened on well-oiled hinges.

Davina stood watching me, wearing a filmy white peignoir tied at her neck. The look in her eye made me feel as though I'd been caught with my hand in the jam jar.

"What are you doing, Sammy?"

"Leaving."

"Don't be silly."

"It's not silly. It's the best idea I've had in weeks."

She shut the door behind her, taking a big, resigned breath that pulled the gauzy top of the peignoir tight across her breasts. The nipples were beginning to sprout underneath.

She looked up at me, her eyes big and shiny. "Sammy, I'm sorry I got you into this."

"So am I."

"You shouldn't be involved." She sighed and looked away. "I'm beginning to think none of us ought to be here."

I stepped down off the bed. "Then let's go."

She looked around sharply, her green eyes slightly surprised. "You'd take me with you?"

Her emphasis on certain words gave them a whole different meaning. I opened my mouth to say yes, but nothing came out.

She laughed, but it was more sad than happy. "I wouldn't, even if you asked me, Sammy." She lifted her chin slightly. "Howard and Caleb are family."

"That's the best reason to leave them I can think of."

"They need me. And I need them."

"None of you need me."

She spun around angrily, walked to the door, and flung it open. "There it is. Go on. It would serve you right."

I went to the door and looked out.

"What did you expect?" said Davina.

"Father Christmas, for all I know. Every time I try something original I end up doing exactly what the Williamsons figure I'll do."

"I warned you."

"Where's Caleb?" I said, ignoring the remark.

"I'm not telling." She looked away, then back again, her face a little softer. "I don't know, Sammy. Really."

"If you didn't want me to walk through this door, why did you unlock it?"

Her gaze dropped away. "I didn't want to be alone tonight. I was lonely."

"You've been alone all week. And avoiding me to boot."

"I had to," she said quickly. "Come on, I'll show you why."

She took my hand and pulled me along the hall to the other wing of the farmhouse. She opened a door and went in. I still expected Caleb behind the door grinning and telling me I'd been suckered again.

"Oh, come on," she said, exasperated.

The room was almost identical to mine. Plain heavy oak bed without a headboard. Straight-backed chairs, and a mirrored wardrobe standing next to a low washbasin without benefit of plumbing. Except from a beam across the ceiling hung a length of knotted nylon rope of the same kind I'd seen on the workbench in the servants' quarters.

"Why the rope?"

She hesitated a moment, then smiled. "I'll show you."

She turned her back to me and began tugging at the neck of her peignoir. "Here, hold this."

Suddenly the peignoir was in my hand, Davina's well-formed all-together reflected in the mirror.

Davina dressed had only hinted at what might be underneath. Her body was perfect, full and round, but the flesh taut, with dimples and perfectly sculptured lines where the separate parts of her torso joined.

She moved toward the rope without self-consciousness. "Now watch."

She reached forward, wrapping her fingers around the rope almost in a caress, each hand just above the knot, about two feet apart.

Then she raised up on her toes, tensed, and without seeming to exert any effort pulled her legs up in a slow sweep until they paralleled the floor, her slender arms supporting her body rigidly but without strain. With her legs held out straight on either side of the rope, toes pointed, slowly, and under complete control, she went arm over arm up to the beam, and down again at the same speed.

While I stared like the village idiot, she did it again.

I don't know if it was the taut perfection of her body, or the grace of her movements, or a weird combination of the two. Davina climbing that rope created a hollow excitement way down below my belt that didn't come along very often. I've seen an X film or two, flipped the pages of those Danish skin mags, even had a fling once with a lady gymnast on a mirrored opium bed I still think about. But the sight of Davina on that rope etched itself in my brain to stay.

She dropped lightly to the floor and grinned at me, one hand still touching the rope. "A week ago I could barely do that a half dozen times. Now I can go up twenty, twenty-five times without stopping. I've been practicing, doing special exercises."

"Practicing for what?"

The smile changed ever so slightly. The cool night air had put a layer of fine goose bumps across Davina's breasts and shoulders, and her nipples had turned pointy and hard.

She let go of the rope and walked toward me slowly, chin high, shoulders back, the smile changing again to something not quite so secret. Her eyes slid away from mine, focusing on something behind me, and for a jumpy second I thought it might have been Caleb.

I turned around. The only thing there was the big oak-framed bed, looking about the size of an aircraft carrier.

Davina's arms wrapped around me from behind, and her mouth came close to my ear. "Do you suppose it's as sturdy as it looks?"

Sometime later, when the single candle Davina had lighted burned down, and old Sammy along with it, she moved around on her hip and snuggled back against me.

There was a faint light in the room that must have been starlight from an absolutely cloudless sky. The silence was deep enough to wade in.

Without really wanting to, I found myself thinking about what Manning Able had said about making a success of something big enough to satisfy whatever demon it was chasing around inside me.

Papa Victor had always been a great believer in luck. And that luck, good or bad, eventually changed. When it was good, Sammy, he'd say to me, push it for all it's worth because you're only going to have it good for so long. It all sounded a bit Oriental, but I'd spent too much time inside a gambling house to believe there was no such thing as a lucky run. The guys that had the balls to press it were the winners in this world.

My problem is I'd never been able to tell the end of a good run from the start of the bad, and let me tell you how fast you can hit bottom pressing a losing bet. But there with Davina, in a length of time that wouldn't have fitted in a second, I knew with a certainty rare in my life that somewhere, somehow, a big chance was coming. I hoped I recognized it when it happened.

Of course, if I blew the whole thing and lived through it, I'd go back and drive a stake through Victor's coffin.

When Davina spoke, I realized she was wide awake and thinking, too. "We're a long way from where we began, aren't we, Sammy?"

"You and me?"

"That too. I was thinking of Howard and me. Even Caleb. We were carnies, the Williamsons, going way back." Her voice was soft and a little tired. "When Howard and I were still kids, carnival was already dying. Even I was old enough to know if we didn't get out we'd rot. Finally it got so bad the family was driving four hundred miles a day, working dinky county fairs, then sitting out winter wondering if come spring there'd be any work at all."

She took in a long, deep breath and let it out slowly, ending with a low, distant laugh.

"Caleb was first to get out. A job in the rock quarries. Then, when he found he played a good hand of cards, traveling the circuit. Caleb knows every stud-poker city between Globe and Wheeling." She added with a certain pride, "What Caleb did, he did himself, Sammy."

"Nothing would surprise me. What about you and Howard?"

She hesitated a long time before she answered. "I was eleven and Howard twelve when our parents died. A semi lost its brakes on a stretch of road just east of Evansville, Indiana, and sliced through the pickup truck with them in it. Howard and I were in the trailer they were towing. After that Howard went to live with Caleb. I was raised by Ma's sister." She sighed, her eyes fixed on the ceiling. "I guess Caleb tried."

"Tried what?"

"To keep Howard out of it. Caleb made him attend regular school, then footed the bill for the university.

Howard's got a couple of degrees in things I can't even pronounce. Had a nice clean job up in an office in Chicago, wearing a necktie and everything. Stuck with it almost five years. I guess it pretty nearly killed him off." She shook her head sadly. "Poor Howard."

I could have told her Howard was dead last on my list of people to feel sorry for. "Poor Howard," I said, and stroked Davina's silky hair, poured out across the pillow next to me like spilled cream.

"There must be something about Williamson blood." She moved her head from side to side, bewildered. "One day he showed up on Caleb's doorstep, suitcase in hand, and said he wanted to learn the business."

"What business?"

"Oh, by then"—Davina hummed evasively—"Caleb was doing this and that."

What she said next came out with the bitterness I'd heard briefly that first day riding in the MG. "I got out the easy way. At fifteen I ran off with the first man who got up my skirt. A big, foxy talker who was going to take me places I'd never been. He did that all right. Billie Bob Hardesty and the Bandling Brothers Circus and Tent Show. One ring, and the permanent smell of animal-dung and mildewed canvas, guaranteed to stay in your nose until you die."

"You don't have to tell it, Davina," I said, but she wasn't listening.

"I learned aerial work from Billie Bob, yes, sir, and a lot of other things I'd like to forget." She leaned up on one elbow quickly, a hardness behind Davina's eyes I should have taken note of. "I'll tell you one thing, Sammy. I'm not ever going back to that. Nothing like that. I'll stick my head in an oven before I end up old and poor. I don't ever want to be poor again."

"Hey, now," I said, and reached out. She moved closer, and then she was pulling herself toward me with sort of a wild urgency. Close, she smelled like musky soap, and her skin was hot and smooth. "Hang onto me, Sammy," she said in a way that left no room for argument. "Oh, Sammy, please."

The idea of arguing hadn't entered my mind.

Later I went off in a deep, dark sleep that should have lasted a dozen hours. The next thing I knew I was wide awake again, pulled up with a start.

It was still dark, and for a moment I didn't know where I was. I felt Davina next to me, breathing rhythmically, and remembered with mixed feelings.

The niggling thought that kept poking its way into my mind was, if Davina hadn't walked into my room the exact minute I was about to climb out the window, I'd be miles away and moving fast.

Considering the ways in which we'd passed the time after that, I couldn't understand why I'd woken up at all.

Then I realized the night's silence was no longer absolute. In the distance I heard the low whine of an automobile driving in low gear, then another. I slid out of bed quickly, stuck my feet into my shoes and grabbed clothes in handfuls.

By the time I was back in my room, up on the bed and looking out, the place was beginning to sound like Brands Hatch in July.

Moving along the drive toward the farmhouse were four sets of dimmed headlights.

I recognized the first car as it drove into the courtyard as the SEAT 850. The next two cars pulled in behind it and then maneuvered themselves around the yard until they were facing out again. It looked almost military.

My stomach had been all right until then. The men who stepped from the cars were so many black shapes. I counted ten, including the unmistakable stumpy figure of Caleb.

Then the fourth car pulled into the courtyard, a gray grime-covered Renault 16. When the door opened, the interior light blinked on. Howard was behind the wheel, with one other man in the front seat. I'd never seen him before. I knew it would be a long time before I'd forget his face. It was flattened almost unnaturally, the broad, thin mouth stiffened into a permanent grin.

The face belonged to Emile Coudert. Formerly Major Emile Coudert, Armée Nationale Congolaise, and a few other small wars since then.

11

A rough hand shook me out of sound sleep. "Wake up, Samuel." A pale dawn lit the room. Howard was standing over me.

"Don't you ever sleep?" I said.

Dark circles ringed Howard's eyes. "No time," he said jumpily. "Come on, we have guests. I want you to make breakfast."

"Señora Muñoz won't like that."

"Señora Muñoz is gone. The less said about her, the better. Davina will help you."

It was the most heartening news I'd had in days. I went down to the kitchen, washed the taste of the morning out of my mouth with fresh orange juice, and went to work.

The pantry was filled with foods of all kinds, so it wasn't as though the arrival of guests had been unanticipated by Señora Muñoz.

I made a large pot of coffee, laid out two dozen eggs, and cut up several loaves of crusty local bread. It felt good to be in a kitchen again.

Davina came in a few minutes later. Her face had a healthy glow, but the hard, troubled look was back in place around her eyes.

She avoided looking at me directly. She went straight to the cupboard and began laying out plates in a precise row along the counter top that separated the kitchen from the dining room.

I have the utmost respect for the varied roles of women in the modern world. But I can't stand them in the kitchen.

"Davina, I'll do it," I said. "Why don't you take a long hot bath or a nap or something?" I meant it.

She looked up at me quickly, anger flaring. "Oh, Sammy, don't be such a good guy." She was still glaring at me when the six of them walked in.

I don't know what I expected, but they weren't exactly a surprise. Washed out, hollow-eyed old men, all stamped from the same mold, although I doubted if any of them were older than thirty. They shuffled in, dragging their feet, wearing faded khaki fatigues, and looking around nervous-eyed. None of them took a second look at Davina, which wasn't natural.

When I served their food, they went at it like machines, gulping black coffee, smoking and muttering while they ate in a monosyllabic Belgian French not native for several of them.

The stiff, grinning character I'd seen the night before wasn't among them. By my count that still left four new arrivals to come.

The two who came in next were locals, wiry Spaniards with sharp, quick eyes, dressed in loose-fitting clothing. They drank coffee heaped to the brim with sugar, dipping the bread into it and stuffing their mouths while they talked. The other six might not have been there. They jabbered loudly in a brand of Andalusian Spanish that seemed to be without any consonants at all.

Their obvious lightheartedness made the others all the more sullen. I expected we could have had our own private battle if Caleb and the man with the stiffened grin hadn't walked in at that moment.

Caleb moved heavily, as though still partially asleep. The other walked upright as a rod, slapping an ebony swagger stick in the palm of one hand. The Spaniards barely looked up. The men in fatigues stood mechanically until they were dismissed with a perfunctory wave of the swagger stick.

A frozen gaze took in the Spaniards, slipped past me, and stopped on Davina. In the light his face wasn't any more pleasant than it had been the night before. The whole left side stayed rigid no matter what the right side chose to do. The skin had a glossy look, the features flattened as though someone had given them a push before they were fully set. Whatever had wiped out the original couldn't have left much to work with.

"And who is this young lady?" His English was heavily accented.

"My niece," said Caleb slowly. "Howard's sister. Davina, meet Major Coudert."

"Charmed," said Coudert, extending a hand. Davina met it and immediately went rigid. Coudert bent from the waist and kissed her hand at some length. I could smell his cologne then, a heavy flowery potion scented with what the French call frangipani. I'd be off the smell of it for life. Still holding Davina's hand, Coudert said, "A pleasure, mademoiselle. Your beauty helps to offset the roughness of this." He made a sweep of the dining room with his swagger stick.

Davina tried to smile.

"You better have coffee if you're going to." Caleb's voice was measured and flat. He'd noticed Coudert's appraisal and hadn't liked it any better than I had.

Coudert nodded and ordered what he wanted in crisp, demanding tones, without really looking at me.

Another stunt like the hand-kissing and I'd have a laxative in his scrambled eggs.

At exactly eight o'clock Howard arrived with another Spaniard. He was taller and younger than the other two. Howard introduced him as Cruz. That made the lot. An even dozen, including Howard, Caleb, and Major Coudert.

"I congratulate you, Williamson," said Coudert. "I hope the rest of your plans show as much forethought." He slid an oily gaze around at Davina.

Howard and Caleb exchanged slim glances. Howard's manner was tighter than ever. "You'll find our planning adequate, Major. Have your men in the servants' quarters in ten minutes."

Before Coudert could reply, Howard spun around and

walked out of the dining room. Coudert watched him leave, a mirthless grin on his stiffened face.

When they'd gone, I cleaned off the tables quickly. Davina was pecking around the sink, doing very little except sliding plates around. She was pale as a sheet.
"None of us liked Coudert's performance, Davina."
"His face is plastic. It's cold, and those lips. . . ."
I told her to wash up and to make sure the dishes had a double hot rinse. What I really felt like doing was giving her a good squeeze. At that moment it would have been like putting a hand on a drunk. Most will stay upright until they know they have someone to lean on; then zip, they go floppy on you every time. There are some things that don't get any better by talking about them anyway, my uncle used to say. That was usually just before he unloaded on you whatever was bothering him at the moment. Besides, I had something to do. Leaving Davina with something else on her mind made it a little easier.

When I was sure the pack of them were all inside the servants' quarters, I went around to the back. I went straight to the window I had climbed through the day before. I had thought about that window from the minute Howard had told Coudert to assemble his men.
When I'd jimmied it open I'd sprung the hinges, thereby slipping one-half of the latch loose from the half fitted deeply into the oak window frame.
The window was askew on its hinges, but almost shut. I eased it open inch by careful inch until it was at a forty-five-degree angle, although cock-eyed a bit. I thought by doing so I'd be able to use the window as a mirror, viewing in profile a good slice of the room where Coudert's men were waiting for whatever good word Howard was to give them. Stunts like that only happen in movies. When I'd done it, I couldn't see a bloody thing.
I looked around for another way to see what was happening. If I didn't find out what this business was about,

I knew somehow I'd end up in a worse bind than I was at the moment.

Two feet to the left of the window and slightly higher, I saw it. A rectangular frame set in the plaster, with ceramic louvers maybe a foot in width. It must have been near the stove, a vent to let out the heat of the kitchen.

I stood on my toes and peeked through it at a bigger slice of the room than I could have seen from the window.

At that moment Howard walked briskly into the picture and moved to the front of the room. He seemed strung as taut as a bowstring, and I had the feeling again his appearance of absolute confidence was as much an act of will as anything else. He carried a thick folder and a rolled chart of some kind.

The moment he put the folder on the table and looked up, Coudert's men stopped talking. One folded his hands under his armpits. Another let his eyelids droop skeptically. I hoped Howard could carry it off. They were a bunch of hungry animals watching something that might very well end up their supper. One sign of weakness and they'd pounce.

The three Spaniards looked on blankly, one picking his teeth with a pocket knife. The one named Cruz had no expression at all.

Caleb moved himself to the side of the room. It was getting so that I could read his poker face. At the moment he was as close to nervousness as he probably could be.

A frozen grin settled on Coudert's face. He looked at Howard with the arrogance of a man who had seen it all and thought nothing could surprise him.

When Howard spoke, I realized I'd have no trouble hearing what he said. I could feel the tension in the room.

"Gentlemen, the fact that we are together in this room signals completion of the first phase of our project."

Howard's enthusiasm didn't exactly stimulate the rest

of them. Coudert's men looked at each other, then in unison turned toward Coudert expectantly.

Coudert cleared his throat and stood. "Now that I am here, Williamson, am I to understand that you intend to remain in command?" His meaning was clear to everyone. He was, after all, the military man.

Howard didn't seem flustered by Coudert's remark. "Let's clear one thing up right now." His voice was pleasant enough. "By your use of the word 'command,' I take it you assume we are about to embark on something of a military nature?"

"Judging by the talents of the majority, quite so." Coudert's face had a wooden smirk.

"I grant you I know little about the military, Major. Except they are extravagant of their resources, take unnecessary risks, and, more than that, are grossly inefficient." The sharpness in Howard's voice made cords jump out in Coudert's neck. "I am a businessman, Major. This project is strictly a business venture. As such, it will be conducted solely on the dictates of sound management practice and through use of some rather successful operational techniques."

"You're making yourself the boss then," said one of Coudert's men gruffly. "What's the difference?"

Howard riveted him with a quick glance. "There is no boss. I will give no orders. It is my job to analyze and define. I will outline what must be done, good soldier, and your commander will tell you how. Assuming you follow his orders, there should be no problems. If you must have a name for my role, consider me project director, nothing more."

There was a bewildered muttering from Coudert's men. Coudert was still facing Howard. "If this isn't a military mission, then why the hell are we here?"

"You are being paid to be here, first off," Howard said, smiling thinly. "You and your men are one of four teams necessary to carry out the project. All the teams have specialized activities. Yours will be military in nature. By the time you leave this room you'll know exactly what those activities will be. If you'll allow me, that is, Major."

Howard straightened, looking taller and leaner than usual. Caleb's eyes fixed on a point about a foot over Coudert's head. Coudert glanced from one to the other, then at the Spaniard named Cruz who looked back with the deadest expression I'd ever seen. Coudert grunted and sat down reluctantly. Round one to Howard.

Howard appeared to take no notice. "The purpose of any business venture is to make a profit. Therefore any profit-making venture must have an objective worthy of the risk." Howard opened the folder on the table in front of him. "Please note, gentlemen.

"One. Luis Miguel Borrasa. Spanish, aged fifty-eight. Principal owner of Minas Borrasa, Aeronaves del Sur, and the Solimar Transportation Company S.A., registered in Panama City, a fleet of some eighteen ships. The London *Financial Times* ranks Borrasa as the twenty-second richest individual in the world, with a personal fortune in excess of three hundred million dollars. Borrasa once referred to himself merely as a very successful collector. You have noticed the island several miles off the coast. Its name is Tiburón. It is owned by Borrasa, and on it he has built an imposing home, the Villa Joyosa."

Coudert was working himself up to say something, but Howard kept going.

"Two. Nikolides Girondas. Greek-born, Argentine citizenship. Aged sixty-eight. Shipping, meat-packing, Argentine real estate. He has dabbled in movie producing for its fringe benefits. Personal fortune indeterminate. Assets of majority-owned companies over a billion dollars. Close friend of Borrasa, stemming from the time when they both had a fondness for the same young French film actress.

"Three. Mahmoud Falek. Moroccan, aged forty-seven. Acknowledged business, hotels. Also has interests in brothels in Casablanca and Rabat and reportedly the wholesale trafficking of hashish. Paid income tax on fifty thousand dollars last year. Actual earnings said to be closer to ten times that. At this moment hoping to interest Borrasa in investments.

"Four. Gerhard Schiller. Swiss, aged sixty. Director of the Hispano-Suisse Merchant Bank, A.G. Zurich. Reputedly assured his fortune by actively luring deposits from wealthy European Jews prior to World War Two, assets his bank now uses at will. Gold trader, connoisseur of the arts, a confessed epicure. Assets: for all practical purposes unlimited. Close friend and financial adviser to Borrasa."

Howard placed the sheet of paper in the folder and looked up.

"Within forty-eight hours those gentlemen and, more important, their wives will be enjoying themselves less than three miles from where you sit. All will be guests of the generous Luis Borrasa for the beginning high season, a no doubt profitable exercise in the art of mixing business and pleasure."

"Oh, come now, Williamson," Coudert snapped peevishly. "Wealth is always impressive. But the antics of such people are suitable only for the twittering of newspaper gossip columns. So Borrasa will have guests. What of it? Kidnapping is farfetched and messy. The change in their pockets is scarcely worth robbery. For most of them money is an abstract, simply figures on a balance sheet."

"Hardly, Major." Howard slid a large envelope from the folder. He removed several glossy photographs. "Four, men, four examples."

He held up one of the photographs. One of Coudert's men gave a low whistle.

"This is Leila Falek. Hardly the picture of Muslim modesty. The photo was taken at St.-Tropez last August. She wears a bikini rather well. And frequently. What appears to be a belt around her waist is a gift of two years ago. A simple appreciation of his wife's attractive hips, from Mahmoud. Diamonds, a single strand some twenty-eight inches long. Market value about six hundred thousand dollars. On the parallel market we shall be using, about one-third that."

"And you're counting on her bringing the diamonds to the Villa Joyosa?" Coudert's voice was scornful.

"She wore them last year at St.-Tropez, and this March at Carnival in Rio. The odds are good." Howard shrugged. "Hardly worth worrying about either way. Example two."

Howard showed another photograph.

"A tiara of diamonds and emeralds. The Señora Schiller is Colombian. Ninety percent of the world's emeralds come from Colombia, a good portion of them brokered by Señora Schiller's father. The tiara was a gift on her twenty-first birthday. The stones are flawless as one might expect. I am assured the tiara can be broken up, reset, and, if patiently disposed of, sold at about half their current value."

"And I suppose Señora Schiller will wear this with her bikini?" There was dutiful laughter from Coudert's men, but most of them kept their eyes riveted to the photo.

"In an interview in the Brazilian magazine *Manchette*, Señora Schiller mentioned she wears it for good luck each birthday, a not uncommon bit of Latin sentiment. A lucky coincidence you might say."

"Oh?" said Coudert.

"Her birthday occurs during the stay at the Villa Joyosa. She has the tiara with her, heavily insured, of course. A bonus for our effort. Example three."

Howard held up another photograph.

"In such company this must look the pauper. A simple diamond necklace, a wedding gift from Girondas to his now fat but contented Greek wife, given at a time when he struggled toward his second million. She could have ten like it now at the wave of a finger. She prefers this because she too is sentimental. It is the only jewelry she owns. Value, about two hundred and fifty thousand dollars. Worth one-third that if fenced properly. There is a good likelihood however that Mrs. Girondas would consider buying her necklace back at a rather increased price. Our broker won't be greedy." Howard looked at Coudert. "I hope the sight of diamonds isn't boring you, Major?"

"The prospect of money never bores me, Williamson. I am still reluctant to base an entire 'project,' as you call it, on the chance that these jewels will be present."

"Nor would I. The discovery of that likelihood was made in the normal course of research. Example four is our insurance." He showed the last photograph. "Also a wedding present. From Borrasa to his new bride of now six weeks, Sylvia. A woman of great beauty, I am told. That is not a chicken egg, gentlemen. It is the Frederika Diamond, a flawless South African yellow. Weight, three hundred and seventeen carats. Bought on behalf of Borrasa at auction from Sotherby's one year ago for eight hundred thousand pounds, about two million dollars. Resale value, absolutely zero."

Half of Coudert's face whitened. "What do you mean?"

"I mean the diamond is one of a kind. If it were stolen, no one could wear it without immediately being identified as the thief. Broken up and recut, it would be worth a fraction of its price."

"Then what good is it?"

"I would have thought none. Until I was informed after discreet enquiries that a certain collector would pay half a million dollars' cash for the knowledge that in his private collection he has the Frederika Diamond. It is at this moment in a rather sturdy safe in the Villa Joyosa."

Coudert's men were beginning to shift in their seats with excitement. The Spaniards sat impassively, as though the trinkets Howard had been showing were so many pebbles.

A crooked smile bent Howard's mouth. "If you have been paying attention Major, you'll have noticed the minimum market value of only these pieces is something over a million dollars. The Frederika Diamond alone would make our project worthwhile. But note I said minimum."

Coudert's men stopped moving, their faces turned forward. "Go on, Williamson," Coudert said without inflection.

"I haven't bothered to mention the assorted pieces of jewelry, the wedding rings, the gold, the precious objects of art, and the very real possibility of considerable cash in the possession of Borrasa and his guests. A half million dollars is our budgeted minimum, gentlemen. A more realistic figure might be to add another one million. If we are lucky, perhaps twice that. That's what we intend to do, gentlemen. Take the Villa Joyosa and sack it for everything it's worth." Howard slid his eyes around the room quickly. "Are there any other questions about our objective?"

12

They sat staring at Howard, not a stunned muscle moving on any of them. Coudert broke the spell.

"You've painted an enticing picture, Williamson. As you can tell, you have captured the imagination of my men. I'm not so ready to jump on the bandwagon."

"I'd never thought of this as a bandwagon."

Coudert's voice was smug. "Any man with combat experience would appreciate the complexity of the tactics necessary to raid an island and separate those jewels from their owners. Call it the skepticism of an old soldier."

"Any competent operations analyst would find the whole exercise primitively simple."

The atmosphere in the room went tense. "Simple?" said Coudert, unbelieving. "Don't be ridiculous."

"Major, the only thing keeping us from those diamonds is exactly thirty-eight definable 'events,' as I prefer to call them. Each event is completed by performing a series of activities which can and have been precisely described. At this moment we have already completed twelve events. Our project is nearly one-third finished."

Howard's eyes worked around the room, a genuine confidence growing each minute.

"I'm listening," said Coudert.

I was more than listening. I was shaking all over. The sight of that mammoth diamond changed my life.

"I hope you listen well, Major," Howard was saying. "Those thirty-eight events have been neatly laid out in a network plan, which is nothing more than a schematic diagram of the raid. Using a computerized program evaluation review technique—a PERT program we call it in my business—I determined among other things the activity times needed to complete each event. It was like shooting a mouse with an elephant gun, but it was an interesting exercise. Compared with programming the London rail system or building a prototype Polaris missile, both of which employed similar techniques, the raid on the Villa Joyosa is an exercise for kindergarten children. All you must do, Major, is complete your assigned events by performing the activities in the time budgeted you. I have taken pains to assign you only activities within your stated competence. Do that, and three days from now you and your men will be richer than you have ever been."

Without hesitating, Howard hung the chart on the wall and let it unroll with a crack. Lettered on the first page were the words "Raid at Tiburón," and then in parentheses in bold letters PROJECT RAT.

"If you have no other comments, Major, I'd like to get on with it." It was an open challenge.

"Please do," said Coudert, trying to sound as though he were giving Howard leave. But the tide had turned, and everyone in the room knew it. Coudert's men were watching Howard as though his words were the equivalent of gold sovereigns.

"Later today each team leader will receive computer print-outs with his assigned events, the activities necessary to complete them, and the allowable maximum and minimum activity times necessary to stay on schedule." Howard nodded toward the chart. "Outlined here are the obstacles and variables of the project as a whole."

"Well, at least you admit there are obstacles."

"Of course there are, Major. These were defined during the research stage and have been planned for. The variables are largely within our control. Even the human factors, which is the likely place where snags might occur, have been taken into account. You and your people will have a large role in creating an environment where human reactions can be predetermined with fair accuracy. In any case, I've made contingency plans for a number of different scenarios." Howard turned to the chart. "The project site is something we must all deal with."

He flipped over a page on the chart to reveal a drawing. Coudert leaned forward in his chair. From the general shape of the drawing I could tell it was the bay on the seaward side of Tiburón, considerably enlarged over the map I'd seen at the British Museum.

"And what exactly are we looking at?" asked Coudert.

"The site of the Villa Joyosa. This kidney-shaped bay is located on the southern side of Tiburón. At the top of the kidney here," Howard said, pointing, "is the villa itself. This line you see leading from it around the perimeter of the bay is a stone-paved road, approximately eight feet in width and a mile or so in length. There are four guest villas spaced along the road and slightly above it. The other buildings you see are servants' quarters and auxiliary buildings. The sides of the bay rise rather steeply. These paths leaving the main road slope down to the beach but nowhere have an incline greater than fifteen feet per hundred feet. There are no automobiles on the island."

"One," said Caleb from a corner.

"Correction. A twenty hundredweight Land Rover. Each villa is equipped with an electric cart which is used to spare Borrasa's guests the effort of walking either the hundred yards or so to the beach or to the Villa Joyosa. As for the beach itself, mostly pebble, except for the area directly adjacent to the boathouse. That section is fine white sand, brought in several times a year by barge from Morocco."

"Irrelevant observation, I'm sure," said Coudert.

"Unless your men choose to move along the beach. In which case the noise they make will be alarm enough. A single person walking over those pebbles would be heard for several hundred feet."

Coudert made a slight bow. "I'll remember your advice."

"Not advice, Major. I'm offering you only information. As I said, specific tactics will be left up to you."

"We'll try to measure up to your confidence." Coudert's voice was without humor. He pointed to the drawing with his swagger stick. "In front of the Villa Joyosa. Your map indicates a building. What is it?"

"A boathouse reached either from the beach, the road, or via cable car from the villa. There will be two boats moored inside. One is a forty-two-foot gasoline-powered yacht, recently renamed the *Sylvia* in honor of the new Señora Borrasa. The other is an eighteen-foot open launch used as a ferry between the bay and the mainland. Otherwise, the site is physically isolated, which is exactly as Borrasa intends it."

"He must have communications," said Coudert.

"Telephone and teletype via a special cable. There is also radio equipment in the villa. You don't run a worldwide empire like Borrasa's over the phone. I've listed these as obstacles under our control."

"Under our control?" he questioned.

"They are inanimate objects, Major. We'll have neutralized communications before the actual raid begins."

Coudert started to protest. "I can't get my men inside—"

Howard cut him off. "You don't have to get your men anywhere. I said there would be four teams. You and your men are the Red Team. Destroying communications is the task of the Yellow Team, event sixteen to be precise. The second obstacle under our control more directly concerns you. The matter of timing. Caleb will explain."

Caleb shuffled to the front of the room, prodding tenderly at the back of his neck. "Most of the guests are scheduled to arrive at the Villa Joyosa the day after tomorrow. The problem was when to hit them. We calculated there were only two times that made any sense. One, when they were together, maybe at dinner that first night. Everyone is all dolled up and in one place, the Villa Joyosa. Except that has as many drawbacks as advantages."

"Enumerate, please," pecked Coudert.

"It will be night. Which means it will be a lot harder to keep track of everyone. We're liable to need eyes in the back of our heads anyway."

"What do you mean?" one of Coudert's men piped up nervously.

Howard replied, "Only that we have to account for more people than Borrasa and his guests. There'll be a number of servants and so forth." It was Howard's style of understatement again; I bet there was more to it than he was letting on.

One-half of Coudert's face warped into a frown. "Perhaps you'll elaborate."

Coudert was no fool, and I hoped Howard knew it.

Howard fielded it without hesitating. "There is an estate guard of three men. They are armed with sidearms and shotguns, never fired in anger apparently. If surprised and overwhelmed quickly, they should provide little resistance. Juapa may be more troublesome."

"The word means handsome in Spanish, does it not?" asked Coudert.

"Spelled differently, it does. And in reference to anybody else. Juapa is Borrasa's chauffeur, valet, pimp, and bodyguard, all in one very ugly bundle. He's armed and will shoot if given a reason. Three years ago in Barcelona he beat to death a Czech playboy while supposedly protecting Borrasa. From what, the papers never quite said. He is dangerous in any case."

Caleb deftly steered the discussion in another direction. "As I see it, the main problem with robbing everyone together is we still have to go through each of the guest villas or risk losing a good part of the loot. You can only wear so many diamonds at once. Besides, someone who gets robbed in front of his friends is all the more likely to get showoffy, especially with a couple of drinks under his belt. Once a commotion starts it ain't easy to stop without someone getting hurt."

"We must minimize the unpredictable," Howard said.

"The alternative is perfectly clear," said Coudert arrogantly. "We must attack them separately and when they least expect it. Divide and conquer."

"Exactly, Major. Red Team events twenty, twenty-one, and twenty-two." Howard smiled. "Your men will take the guest villas and relieve the tenants of their possessions beginning exactly twenty minutes before sunrise three days from now, at 0504 hours to be exact. At that time Borrasa's guests should be in a cooperative mood."

"The guest villas?" Coudert smiled. "My team laps up the milk while the cat gets the cream, is that it?"

"I assume you mean the Villa Joyosa?"

"The Frederika Diamond is in the villa, is it not?"

"Yes, in a safe, a very high quality American-built Hermann. If one of your men can get into it, you're welcome."

"Don't be absurd."

"Caleb can," Howard said matter-of-factly. "Caleb and I will make up the Blue Team."

"And how will he do this?"

"I'm sure Caleb would refer to himself as nothing but 'an old-fashioned powderman.' I assure you he could blow a fly off a window without breaking the glass."

"Now, Howard, that's exaggerating some," said Caleb modestly. "But not much."

"If Caleb had time, he could probably take the safe apart so neatly it could be fitted together again. We don't have the time. For reasons I'll come to we must finish the operation at the villa by 0700."

"What he's trying to tell you," said Caleb, "is I got to blow the hell out of that safe. Quick and dirty we say in the trade. Your boys want to stand around and watch, that's fine by me. Frankly, I find that kind of blasting a little risky."

"Very well. But we intend to assure that all has gone well."

"Event number twenty-six," Howard said. "All teams assemble at the villa."

"Is there anything else?" Coudert asked acidly.

"Yes, there is, Major. In addition to carrying out your

events, you and your men have one other assignment."

"Are you sure we are qualified?"

"Perfectly. You must provide the illusion of danger."

Coudert gave a sarcastic grunt. "I would think this project dangerous enough."

"There is risk, I suppose. For us it is small. I was thinking of our victims," said Howard. "By event number twenty-six there will be exactly forty-three people under our control, including servants. If we lose that control, their sheer numbers will present a danger. But if we can keep people separated and frightened, then we aren't dealing with a mob. We have small isolated groups ignorant of what may be happening to others and docile to the point of predictability."

"And how do you propose to do that?" Coudert asked.

"I've told you, my job is not to answer how. We have gathered a considerable store of arms and ammunition. I'm sure you'll work out appropriate techniques."

"We might at that," Coudert said, a new interest in his voice.

"We intend to help," said Caleb.

"Yes?" Coudert still sounded as though he were thinking of something else.

Howard said, "As a signal to begin, we plan to blow up the launch."

"Sort of set the tone of things right off." Caleb grinned.

Coudert shrugged. Howard looked at him directly. "There is one thing to remember, Major."

"Only one? I'm gratified."

"We need only the illusion of danger. Dead and wounded on our hands would be a distinct liability."

"Of course," said Coudert evenly. "But in the case things get out of control. . . ."

"Make sure they don't." Howard's voice was sharp.

There was a long silence before Coudert grinned back at Howard and changed the subject. "Perhaps you'll tell me about the guest villas."

"What about them?"

"You mentioned there were four. Borrasa's guests will occupy only three. Which one will be empty, and who will be occupying each of the others?"

"Until they arrive, there is no way of telling. I don't see what difference it makes."

"I have six men to take three villas, plus provide this 'illusion of danger,' as you call it. Some of those guests are likely to be more troublesome than others. Since the choice of tactics is mine, I have plans for the empty guest villa. I therefore must know."

Howard agreed quickly. "You're absolutely right. We'll find out."

"I don't deal in uncertainties," Coudert said, quick to sense he'd found something about which Howard wasn't totally informed.

"Nor do I," Howard snapped. "We'll find out."

One of Coudert's men, a big, lumpish creature, raised a lazy hand. "What about the noise?" he asked, in stilted English.

Coudert seemed pleased. "Sergeant Klug is right. What about noise. Won't the explosions and shooting be heard in La Boca?"

"The possibility was analyzed in the research phase. Detailed weather records at Almería go back only twenty years or so. The climate is classified by Köppen as hot-summer Mediterranean. It is a stable, fairly predictable climate, especially in the summer, and dominated mainly by tremendous heating in the Sahara. That time of the morning there should be an offshore wind of about five or six miles per hour, carrying any sound away from the mainland."

"But if it doesn't?"

"We have made allowances."

"One of your teams will place cotton in the ears of each of La Boca's residents, no doubt." Nobody smiled.

"A military solution perhaps, Major, but for us unnecessary. We calculated what exactly would happen if gunfire were heard from the direction of Tiburón."

"And what would happen?"

"Nothing. It will be Sunday morning. If past performances are taken into account, there is a likelihood that any festivities at the Borrasa's might include fireworks and go on for days."

"And if it was correctly interpreted as gunfire?"

"The authorities would undoubtedly be alerted. The constabulary in La Boca numbers four men. If they were to be assembled, which would not be an easy task at that hour, and voyage to Tiburón by motorboat, the entire process might take two hours. An unlikely adventure if they thought of actually facing a shootout."

"They would do something."

"Yes they would. Immediately call a detachment of the *guardia civil* from Almería. They would arrive two hours and fifteen minutes later, give or take a few minutes. If they were alerted immediately, again highly unlikely, that would mean arrival at La Boca at 0720 with an added twenty minutes in transport to the island. We must allow for a slight margin of error. That is why we must be finished and off the island by 0700."

"Imaginative theorizing, Williamson, but—"

"Nothing of the sort," Howard cut in. "About six weeks ago a mysterious explosion on the outskirts of La Boca destroyed an abandoned olive press. The local constabulary received a phone call that suggested the place was being used as an explosives drop by Basque separatists moving goods north. The *guardia civil* arrived in exactly two hours and twenty-three minutes. They found nothing but a hole in the ground. Even through binoculars they looked quite puzzled."

"You set the explosion?"

"I thought a dry run advisable."

Coudert's jaw went slack an instant, then tightened. "I hope you've been as careful insuring our exit will not be delayed?"

"We'll arrive and leave the same way, by small boat. That's their job." Howard pointed toward the Spaniards. "Cruz and his men are the third team, the Green. They'll land us in two separate boats between 0200 and 0300 hours. When the operation is finished, we return to the boats. Cruz's men will take us to a point on the mainland where transport will be waiting. We separate there, a portion of your salaries in pocket. The final payment, as we agreed, will be paid into a Swiss account within three months."

One of Coudert's eyes narrowed, the other holding a glassy stare. "How do I know that?"

"You don't. We must broker the goods, so there is no other choice. Since you can identify me and everyone involved, it is a fair risk."

"Not quite everyone," said Coudert. "I count here only members of three teams. Where is the fourth?"

"The Yellow Team will complete its events inside the Villa Joyosa before the rest of us begin."

"Inside the villa," Coudert said, one eyebrow rising. "Of course. I should have realized it. You have people working for Borrasa."

"We will have."

"Competent, I pray?"

"Perfectly, for what they need to do. You may have met the key person this morning."

"The lovely girl Davina." Coudert nodded. "I suspected she had rare talents."

"No, actually, the other one, Samuel, the cook who prepared breakfast."

13

"Samuel, I admit I haven't been completely frank with you." Howard paced the length of one of the farmhouse bedrooms, frowning. Caleb watched me dully over the top of a straight-backed chair, sitting on it reversed.

"To put it mildly," I said angrily.

Howard held up a cautioning finger. "But for a moment, put yourself in my shoes."

"My own are fouled enough, thanks."

"There was absolutely nothing to be gained from explaining every detail to you in London."

"*L'officier dine, et le soldat bouffe.*"

"Speak English, boy," said Caleb.

"The officer dines, the soldier gobbles."

"Samuel," said Howard, stopping, fixing me with a sincere look straight from the Dale Carnegie manual, "I want you to listen to reason."

"Howard, when a conversation starts with that little nugget, there won't be anything reasonable in it. I will not walk into the Villa Joyosa. If you want to threaten me with your stiletto, go ahead. Borrasa and his bodyguard would do worse."

"Nobody is going to threaten you. Here or anywhere else."

"Nobody is going to get me inside Borrasa's villa, either."

Caleb grunted and looked at Howard. "I told you he'd end up costing us."

"Samuel, the risks are absolutely minimal."

"You've spent half the morning telling Coudert the risks. Now suddenly they're minimal."

"The raid will have its share, of course. I meant your part in it." He paused. "It's all been arranged."

"Howard, don't do this to me. I'm not going."

Caleb shrugged and pulled at his ear. Howard sighed. "Then I guess Davina will have to go alone."

"Now wait."

Howard said sharply, "There's no alternative. We need information obtainable only inside the villa."

"And we need a few things done," said Caleb, "that a middling bright chimp could handle."

Howard said, "You won't go. I can't. Caleb can't. Major Coudert and Cruz are unsuitable." He made a tired shrug. "What choice do we have? Davina."

"You expect her to row over in a boat, knock on the door, and say, 'Here I am, can I have a look around?'"

Howard eyed me soberly. "I told you. Cover has been arranged."

"In your mouth that's a sinister word."

"Of course with you out of the picture we'll have to make adjustments. Davina's risk will increase considerably."

"It's all my fault." Both of them stared at me silently. "Okay, Howard," I relented a bit. "What was supposed to happen?"

Howard began pacing again.

"About a month ago, at the insistence of his new bride, Borrasa contacted a well-known Paris agency for the employment of domestics. It seemed that Sylvia felt the household needed a civilizing influence or two. Through the agency, Borrasa contacted and subsequently hired a Mr. and Mrs. Claude Dutreaux. Dutreaux is a chef, superbly qualified and highly recommended. Mrs. Dutreaux is Scottish, skilled in such dignified and genteel household arts as serving tea. They were to arrive at the Villa Joyosa tomorrow in time to prepare for Borrasa's guests."

"Were?"

Howard smiled. "Two weeks ago Sylvia Borrasa changed her mind, evidently a frequently exercised prerogative of the new señora. With appropriate apologies Borrasa wrote Dutreaux, said he would not, alas, be needed and enclosed a check for six months' wages. Dutreaux was puzzled, perhaps. But whatever surprise he had was well compensated for by cash. At this moment the Dutreaux are undoubtedly passing the summer on the Côte d'Azur in a suitably relaxed manner."

I was still one step behind. "So, exit Dutreaux. I don't get it."

"Exit Dutreaux, and enter you and Davina. In their place."

"You just said Borrasa changed his mind."

"The letter received by Dutreaux, over Borrasa's signature, said exactly that."

"You wrote the letter?"

"It amounts to the same thing," Howard said lightly. "Luis Borrasa is expecting a chef and his wife to arrive tomorrow at the Villa Joyosa. He will naturally accept you as the Dutreaux. He will in any case be much too busy to pay attention. Forty-eight hours later you and Davina leave with us. All much, much richer. Simple."

"You'd make walking on water sound simple."

"Not at all." If there was lightness in his tone before, it was gone. "I've examined every aspect of this operation, determined where it might go wrong, then plotted alternatives. I've planned this down to the tick of the clock. Don't forget, Samuel, we have never failed an operation of this kind." The fine print was back in Howard's voice. "All you need do is spend forty-eight hours in the Villa Joyosa, and all will go smoothly."

"What am I supposed to do?"

"How you spend your time matters little. You're nothing more than a Trojan horse to put Davina inside the Villa Joyosa."

"To do what?"

Caleb's poker face was suddenly squarely back in place.

Howard hesitated the barest instant. "We need information. Which guest villa will be empty and so forth."

"Don't forget about the safe," Caleb put in.

Howard blinked. "Ah, yes. Davina must find the precise location of the safe. It could be anywhere, and during the actual raid we won't have time to search for it. Davina will be a very busy girl."

Howard was selling the point very hard. Caleb was watching me with a wary squint. He could have been trying to assess just how easily I'd swallowed what Howard had told me. I had the definite feeling Howard had left something out, but I don't think my suspicion showed. I was beginning to realize Caleb couldn't read my face any better than I could read his, for whatever value it was worth.

"I heard you say the Yellow Team was supposed to destroy communications inside the villa, before the actual raid begins."

"Correct," said Howard. "Telephones, and the radio."

"Davina will do all that, right?"

After a moment's pregnant silence, Caleb said, "Well, no."

"I'm the chimp."

"Take me about a minute to show you. Easy as baking a pie." Caleb realized his mistake. "Easier even."

"Forget it. I'd bungle it."

"If Caleb says he can show you, Samuel, he can."

"It isn't worth the risk."

"For a hundred thousand dollars it is," said Howard. "Full partnership. You could use that kind of money, couldn't you?"

"I could use a pair of wings and a diamond in my navel."

Howard frowned. "What's wrong, Samuel?"

"Only what you're asking me to do. Dutreaux is a master chef. In a household like Borrasa's he does more than stand around with a bonnet perched on his head. He has things to do."

103

"We're in luck there." Howard smiled.

"You think that's lucky?"

"I do. Forty-eight hours isn't long. You shouldn't have to do more than give a few orders."

"Oh?"

"Ibarra will do the work for you."

"Ibarra?"

"Vasco Ibarra. The former chef of the Villa Joyosa. Evidently he has decided to remain, as an assistant. I have reason to believe he was quite competent."

I just looked at him. How anyone could be so smart about some things and so stupid about others I didn't know. It was my turn to pace.

"Howard, there's something you have to understand. Any bunch of experts never agree with each other, do they? I mean disagreement is an absolute necessity. So what makes you think cooks are different? I've seen master chefs fight each other over the proper way to break an egg. Two chefs in the same kitchen are about as stable as sweaty dynamite." Caleb began to look interested. "You think Ibarra is going to be a big help?" I stopped, looked from Caleb to Howard and back again. "Well, it's the worst bloody thing you could have happen. No, Howard," I said, "No, *non*, no."

Caleb slid a glance toward Howard he usually kept reserved for me. Howard ignored it calmly and gave me an understanding smile.

"Now I know what you're thinking, Samuel. That you can't handle it. That it's too big for you."

"That's what I'm thinking."

"But you can. You've spent years in the kitchen. You've learned things, seen things you probably take for granted." He took me by the shoulders. "Samuel, you look and act right. That first night at the Fleur de Lis, we knew you were the man. The one who could pull it off. Didn't we, Caleb?"

"Uh-huh."

I shook loose of Howard and stuck my face toward Caleb. "What do you really think?"

Caleb slowly blinked his puppy-dog eyes at me, and I figured he'd blink about the same way before he broke somebody's neck.

"I think Howard's right," he said slowly. "I hate to admit it to you."

Howard leaned closer. "Borrasa, Vasco Ibarra, all of them have it in their heads the man who arrives is Dutreaux. All you have to do, for forty-eight hours, is be Dutreaux."

Caleb grinned. "A reputation and some hot air go a long way in this world, boy."

It was no use. "And just suppose I get backed into actually preparing something?"

Howard looked puzzled, but only for a minute. "If that happens, then I guess you'll just have to fake it."

14

The infuriating thing about Howard and Caleb was their talent for pulling you in with them. Alone, remembering the Frederika Diamond, I told myself it could work, after all.

Howard's remark about the things I'd experienced in the kitchen had started me thinking. I was even willing to consider, given the circumstances of our arrival at the Villa Joyosa, Davina and I might pass ourselves off as Mr. and Mrs. Claude Dutreaux, for forty-eight hours anyway.

Until I remembered Vasco Ibarra.

What would make a chef with any pride choose to stay behind and work for the new boy on the block?

Perhaps he thought Sylvia Borrasa's passion for things Continental was a passing fad, and when it went so would Claude Dutreaux. Of course if Ibarra discovered Dutreaux was a fraud, it would hasten the process. Vasco Ibarra had the makings of my Jezebel. I hadn't been fooling when I'd told Howard Borrasa and his bodyguard would do worse than use a knife if they found out I wasn't Dutreaux. I could feel it in my bones.

Davina would be even more vulnerable.

Even though Dutreaux's wife was Scottish I wasn't worried about Davina's drawly accent. When you don't speak another language, one accent sounds the same as any other. Unless someone in the Borrasa household spoke fluent English, Davina's accent would be taken for Scottish as easily as anything else.

But Davina spoke no French at all, which married to a Frenchman was unlikely. But then, my mother hadn't spoken a word of French out of pure stubbornness. That shanty-Irish immigrant family of hers considered themselves the equal of anyone, only more so. Speaking any foreign language would have been putting on terrible airs. Anyway, I'd met dozens of Brits living abroad who wouldn't learn the local language on principle.

The real improbability was Davina didn't know the first thing about serving anything. A tea lady, Davina was not.

When I'd finally shaken loose from Howard and Caleb I found Davina, took her to the dining room, and gave her a quick course in serving. Her sense of the practical made it impossible.

"Davina, don't fight it. Serve from the left, no matter what it is. Serve it from the left with your left hand. Remove it from the right with your right hand. Simple?"

"Silly. I'd look funny doing all that walking around."

"You have hundreds of years of convention on your side." On Davina it was a wasted argument. "Just do what I tell you."

"Oh, Sammy," she said, frustrated.

"And when you lean forward, keep your lovely bosoms off the gentleman's shoulder. Many a well-breasted young thing has had her intention misread and ended up serving more than she counted on with sweets in the library."

She glared at me. "I'm not a child."

"Obviously. That's precisely what I'm talking about. I'll try to keep you away from any duties. I don't know. Maybe you should come down with the flu and spend the two days in bed."

"I can't. I have to be able to move around."

"Your assignments won't give you any trouble, will they, Davina?"

"None at all."

I relaxed a little and let out an involuntary sigh. "I'm glad you people know this business cold."

On the way out of the dining room Davina's face had a rigid look that stayed in my mind the rest of the day.

* * *

Major Coudert caught up with me late that afternoon.

He walked into my room without knocking. I was lying on the bed stark naked, studying the computer print-out for PROJECT RAT, trying to read between the lines. I think best flat on my back, preferably in a hot tub. Considering the heat, a tub was the farthest thing from my mind. Sweat was running out of me in small rivers, chasing down my neck, losing itself in the pillow.

"I want a word with you," Coudert said, his good eye surveying me coldly.

"About what, Major?" I got up and slipped on my trousers. It's almost impossible to deal with someone on an equal basis when they are dressed and you're not. I'd already seen the way Coudert operated if he sensed an advantage over you.

"I understand you are Yellow Team leader." His tone said clearly he didn't think much of the idea.

"Correct."

"Your tasks are critically important," he said pompously, "I hope you realize that."

"Of course," I said, without paying him much attention. I was looking for my shoes. When I was dressed, I was getting out of there. The stink of his frangipani cologne was smothering me.

He lifted the edge of the mattress with his swagger stick, glancing under it as a matter of habit. "I wonder if you might run through the Yellow Team events for me." A small black bug climbed over the mattress and made a break for it across the top of the bed.

"Everything's on the print-out."

Coudert watched the bug until it had nearly made it to the crack where the bed met the wall and safety. Then the swagger stick flicked out, and the bug went splat and off into oblivion. "I doubt that."

I looked up to find Coudert watching me curiously. He'd offered me an invitation to share any suspicions I might have had. I wasn't giving Coudert the sweat off my balls. I said, "All except one or two things Davina has to do. The information about who will occupy the three guest villas I believe is for you, Major. What will you do with the empty one?" I tried to make it sound as though I really gave a rat's ass. I found my shoes under the bed and put them on.

His cold eye warmed up a little. "I'll use it as a fire base. Williamson has procured two excellent Belgian FN machine guns. Firing from the guest villa, they will provide"—his voice took on a sarcastic note—"our illusion of danger. Since I have only six men, I plan to bring the guests there as I capture them. One man will have no trouble guarding them." He stopped abruptly. "You were speaking of the lovely Davina."

"That's all. Information, and find the safe."

His good eye narrowed. "They don't know where the safe is?"

"Apparently not."

Coudert pondered it for a moment. "And what will you do?"

"Neutralize communications," I said casually. "Event fifteen."

"When?"

"According to the print-out, I have until 0445 to complete my events, nineteen minutes before your men go into action."

"That's cutting it fine."

"No alternative," I said, repeating exactly what Caleb had told me when I'd made the same comment. "With Borrasa's worldwide business dealings people may try to reach him at any time. Dead communications would arouse suspicion."

"Quite so." Coudert nodded thoughtfully. "And how do you intend to accomplish this task of destruction?"

"I find out after dinner tonight."

"I see."

"Now, if you'll excuse me." I opened the door, walked into the hall, and took in a couple of breaths of fresh air.

Coudert followed me, scratching the dead side of his face with his swagger stick. Part of his mouth started to curl up, and it took me a second to recognize a smile.

"You know, ah, Samuel, I envy one aspect of your assignment. The arrangement with Davina."

"Arrangement?"

"You must appear to be man and wife, eh?" He leered at me. "What better way. . . ." He wiggled the swagger stick back and forth between the thumb and forefinger of his left hand, the grin trying even harder.

"This is strictly business, Major."

"One must take his pleasure when and where he can. With life so uncertain, a man would be a fool to do otherwise. *Bonne chance, mon ami.*"

He gave me a snappy salute, spun, and marched off.

Watching him go, I wondered if his remark had been the warning it sounded. Seeing the last of Coudert was the one good thing about leaving the farmhouse for Tiburón and the Villa Joyosa.

Which Davina and I did, promptly at two thirty in the morning.

Howard drove us in the Renault, along the coast then north into the Sierra, climbing out of the heat to a small town named Guadix. "The train from Madrid stops here a little after five in the morning," Howard explained. "By seven you'll be in Almería, no one the wiser that you didn't come straight through. I had a cable sent in your name from Paris. You'll be met. Probably by Juapa, Borrasa's bodyguard."

He slipped an envelope out of his pocket and handed it to me. "A letter of introduction from the agency in Paris that found Dutreaux. Also a pair of French passports plus a *carte de travail* for both you and Davina under the name Dutreaux. If identification is asked of you, these should suffice."

I took the envelope from Howard without giving him the satisfaction of any comment.

He looked at me in the rearview mirror. "Caleb's briefing on your equipment was clear, I trust?"

"Whoever handles my luggage better treat it with respect."

"Nothing will go off unless you want it to."

Caleb has said the same thing, except he'd been honest enough to add the word "probably." I had one gadget that looked like a small Swiss travel alarm clock with a thick base. It was to go into the junction box of the telephone system, the timer preset for 0445 in the morning. According to Caleb its charge was something called thermite, and it was hot enough when it ignited to fuse the wires in the box in a few seconds.

Caleb had added: "If it were Ma Bell instead of some Spaniard that put in them phones, I'd tell you where to find the junction box, but no can do. You'll just have to snoop."

The two soft plastic envelopes were for the radio. I was to rest them on top of the two largest components, then crush the ampules in the corner of each packet. "That way you'll get either the pre-amp or the side-band transmitter," Caleb had said, "and with not a peep."

"I don't suppose you know where the radio is either?"

"Haven't the foggiest." Caleb had grinned.

When we reached Guadix, Howard parked near the entrance to the railway station and gave us a final, appraising eye.

"Fantastic. Just great."

I wasn't so enthused. Davina wore a plain blue dress with a corsage of small yellow flowers and a hemline a few inches below her knees. She'd pulled her hair around tight behind her head and powdered herself pale. With the loose coat over her dress she looked as close to someone's visiting great-aunt as Davina could. She sat, fiddling nervously with the handle of a large handbag.

For me Howard had picked a suit of stiff tweed, with a cap. I was something out of an old French movie, every American's idea of a peasant shopkeeper, who no doubt fought nights with the maquis. I felt bloody ridiculous. No one had worn suits like that in Paris for three decades, and then not by choice.

It's funny that something as insignificant as a suit of clothing would start me thinking that Howard didn't know as much about anything as he pretended.

"That's it then," said Howard. "Questions?"

"Lots," I said. "How is Davina supposed to get information back to you?"

"Don't worry, Sammy," Davina said. "I'll dream up a reason to go to La Boca when I've found out everything. I leave an envelope at the Hotel Luz in the name of the Señora Muñoz."

"The old crone from the farmhouse?"

"It's just a name," said Howard. "Next question."

"When the raid begins, what's to stop Borrasa or this Juapa from guessing there was inside help and dealing with us before you get there?"

Howard waved the idea aside. "No one thinks about a cook when they're losing a fortune. Besides, there'll be too much confusion. When the shooting starts, stay in your quarters. When we're ready to leave, I'll come for you." He grinned. "Event thirty-six. I think you'll find we've thought of everything."

"Oh, Howard, stop it," Davina said, a sharp bite in her voice.

He added a remark then I should have paid more attention to. "But if things don't appear to happen exactly to plan, don't panic. Trust me, Samuel, and all will end happily."

Papa Victor used to say when a stranger asked you to trust him, you ought to put both hands over whatever it was you valued and exit with haste.

I didn't. I got out of the car with Davina, and we caught the train from Madrid.

15

"You are Dutreaux?"

"I am Monsieur Dutreaux. And this is my wife."

Borrasa's bodyguard straightened at the sharpness in my voice. His dark empty eyes held mine an instant, before he made a clicking sound out of the side of his mouth, as if something had stuck between his wisdom teeth and he was trying to suck it free.

Juapa's name should have been grease. He had long black hair plastered tight against his head, except where it flared out in small curls over the back of his high-roll collar. He was tall, thin-hipped, and slimy. And I didn't like the way he looked at Davina.

"Come." He took Davina's bag and led us through the train station to a long white Mercedes Benz 600 waiting at the curb.

He opened the door and glanced away carelessly as I stooped by him and climbed in after Davina. The door slammed behind me with a smack that very nearly took off my foot. Juapa and I were going to be good friends.

The drive from Almería west along the coast, back to La Boca, was made in absolute silence. Davina smoothed her dress over her knees for the tenth time and squeezed my hand, staring straight ahead. I felt calm and in complete control.

In the train from Guadix while Davina had slept on my shoulder, I'd gone through memories of more kitchens and chefs than I really wanted to think about, searching for elements I could use to create a believable Dutreaux.

Seeing Juapa react to my sharp correction of his lackluster respect made me sure I'd struck upon a couple of traits I'd have no trouble with at all.

As a class, chefs have to be the most quick-tempered people in the world. They may be sweet-faced, nice to their wives, and love animals. But infringe one inch on their sense of worth, and violence is waiting to explode all over you. I understood it. Some people work at jobs where nobody really sees whether they do a lick of real work or not. But a chef lays it on the line, for all to instantly accept or criticize. He's tested every second, and anything that might be interpreted as unjustified criticism or an ever-so-small slight to their ego will provoke a chef's wrath as quickly as flicking a switch.

If I were to be Dutreaux, I had to stay on the offensive, complete with prickly temper and inflated ego. There was no other way to play it.

La Boca turned out to be a small coastal village just far enough from the Almería-Málaga highway to have held out briefly against high-rise apartments and package tour hotels. A Brit would have called it unspoiled. An American would have said quaint.

When Juapa turned the big Mercedes into the entrance of the public pier, I glanced at my watch. The run from Almería had taken just under two hours, a good quarter of an hour less than the estimate Howard had made for the time it would take the *guardia civil* to traverse the distance in case of trouble. But I didn't have time to think about the discrepancy.

We followed Juapa along the pier and down a ramp to the waiting launch. He helped Davina over the gunwale with an oily, swami smile and left me to fend for myself. If callousness was the manner in which the house of Borrasa intended to greet the talented chef Dutreaux, so be it. They would pay in spades.

Just as the launch was casting off, a small boy ran down the ramp and tossed a gray mail sack into the boat.

My new found self-assurance lasted until Juapa piloted the launch out of the lee of the harbor, and we hit the first swell of the open sea. A sailor I'm not. Especially in small, unstable boats.

"You're turning green," Davina whispered. "I didn't think people really did that."

"Keep your observations to yourself."

As we came into the kidney-shaped bay on the south coast of Tiburón, the entire setting was spread out before us. The Villa Joyosa, bigger and more impressive than I'd been prepared for, looking down over a ribbon of road, the beach, and, directly below it, the boathouse. Along the road I could clearly make out the guest villas.

Until that minute it had all been lines and dots on a map, numbered events in Howard's grand plan. Seeing it in stone and concrete made the idea unmistakable; the raid was really going to happen.

Davina must have had the same thought. She took in a small, sharp breath. Her eyes riveted on the Villa Joyosa and stayed there until we'd slid into the boathouse, and Juapa made the launch fast. He dropped over rubber bumpers to fend it off the *Sylvia*, tucked in its berth alongside, and grunted, "This way."

Davina and I followed him through the boathouse, past a door that according to Howard's briefing led to the beach, to a small cable car open from the waist up. Juapa gestured us into the cable car, stepped in behind us closing a gate like a cage door, and pushed a button.

The cable car gave a jerk, and we started up. Juapa's dark eyes moved over Davina to me, and he made that nervous click out of the side of his mouth. He smelled of garlic.

Rising from the boathouse, my eyes followed the pair of steel rails in the direction we were climbing.

At the very top, the rails terminated at a terrace along the second floor of the villa which looked down on the entire setting. I was startled to see a dapper figure dressed in white, behind a large brass mariner's telescope. The telescope pointed down at the cable car. Borrasa.

I shifted my attention to the ground-floor patio just ahead and got a bigger surprise. A crowd was waiting.

I recognized the uniforms, starched aprons and stiff linen jackets. "The household staff," I said.

Davina's eyes followed mine and widened. "What are they doing?"

"We're about to find out."

The cable car slid into a small enclosed house, level with the patio, groaned once, and stopped.

Juapa slid back the gate and pushed open an outer door. "Pass."

Davina and I stepped through it, and for a moment I thought the whole scheme had ended right there.

It was one of those mental pictures you never forget.

Watching us in absolute silence were perhaps a dozen pairs of somber black eyes, above unsmiling mouths. Then the crowd gave way to allow a small, erect man to step forward stiffly.

He was wearing a formal black suit with an absurd puffy handkerchief overflowing from his breast pocket. His lower eyelids seemed to cover the bottom half of his eyes, giving him a permanently sad look. The rest of his face was pinched, from making an effort to keep back a flood of something.

I knew who it was immediately. The chef I'd deposed, Vasco Ibarra.

There was a second an hour long when the only sound was the soft whistle of wind through the leaves of a potted palm.

Ibarra's sad eyes began to water, and he came toward me. He reached out, grasped me firmly with a hand on each shoulder. He bent forward and planted a firm, wet Gallic kiss on each cheek.

A crackle of applause broke out behind him, a bravo or two, and a girl rushed forward and pushed a bunch of roses the size of a hedge into Davina's arms. She took it right in stride, doing a homely little curtsy. Davina could be very, very cool.

"Chef Dutreaux," said Ibarra. The emotion took his

breath before he'd finished the name. He sucked in another. "A great honor, Chef Dutreaux. I am Ibarra. Your humble servant, your eager pupil."

He whisked Davina and me past the household staff to a somber, dark woman a half head taller, whom he introduced as Mrs. Ibarra. Her eyes fixed squarely in the middle of my forehead, and she greeted me without a smile.

If she was less taken by Dutreaux than her husband, that was her concern. The unexpected warmth of our welcome had put me off-balance, like a fighter climbing into the ring expecting to get punched and finding out the other guy hasn't shown up at all. I let Davina and myself be swept along, trying for a moment not to think about Vasco Ibarra's remark, "eager pupil."

Our quarters were just short of luxurious. A separate white stuccoed villa with two large rooms, about twenty yards upslope and behind the Villa Joyosa.

Ibarra led the way up a steep graveled path, talking nonstop in a mixture of Spanish and French and saying nothing more than the Villa Joyosa was honored and elevated by my presence. No one can circumlocute like a Spaniard. Señora Ibarra trailed sullenly behind, saying nothing.

At the doorway to our quarters Ibarra looked at me expectantly. "And when will you inspect the kitchen?"

I needed sleep, a shower, a dozen beers, and about three days to regroup my thoughts. It wasn't, however, Dutreaux's way. I told him now, of course, in a tone that said it had been silly to ask.

I left Davina to unpack. Ibarra and his wife had a brief, sharp exchange I couldn't hear before she marched, heavy-footed, back toward the Villa Joyosa.

Vasco had a pinched look again, which lasted the distance to the kitchen. Once inside his face softened. I recognized the phenomenon. Vasco was home.

The kitchen was a classic rectangle with an alcove for

handling vegetables, two walk-in larders, and a preparation island in the center about ten feet long and half that wide, with storage above it.

We had entered through an outside door that led directly to the graveled path and the chef's quarters. Another pair of double doors led via a short hall to the dining room.

The kitchen staff, looking purposeful and busy when we entered, went stiffly to attention when Ibarra introduced them. The vegetable hand was the same young girl who presented the roses to Davina, a plump, full-hipped creature with a round, angelic face, named Florita.

The kitchen porter was an open-faced man about fifty, with a toothy grin, named Juan. "He's a little . . . you know." Vasco tapped the side of his head. "And sometimes not so good with pots and pans." Vasco gave a shrug. "My brother-in-law."

Every bit of cast iron, aluminum, copper, and stainless steel had been polished and laid out with care. There were enough steamers, kettles, warmers, cruets, casseroles, and paraphernalia to outfit a large hotel.

Almost dancing, Vasco Ibarra led me around the kitchen, flourishing the white handkerchief from his breast pocket, whisking it here and there and flicking it at me, showing it remained clean. He was a very happy man.

"Cleanliness is the soul of the kitchen, Chef Ibarra."

Vasco lowered his eyes demurely and led me toward a pair of huge Wolfe ovens, as though this were the finale.

When he turned, his eyes were glowing a little too brightly. He gave the ovens a loving pat and whispered, bending his head close to them, "We'll see what new Silver Cup will come from these, eh?"

The alarm bells began to ring.

I asked it delicately. "You know of my work, Chef Ibarra?"

"The prize at Biarritz is no secret. Even in Spain."

"And what I cooked, of course, to win the cup?"

"Cooked?" He looked at me blankly.

"Baked," I corrected. "The words in Spanish are unfamiliar."

"Of course." When he led me to one of the larders, he was frowning.

He flung open the door, and we walked in, greeted by the smell of aging meat.

At the end of the larder, low on the wall, was a flat gray metal box. A cable as thick as my wrist led from it, disappearing through the wall. According to Caleb's description it was the telephone junction box that in less than thirty-six hours I was supposed to destroy. It reminded me why I was there, and I was almost sorry.

Walking out of the larder, Vasco Ibarra turned, the frown still on his face.

"A million pardons, Chef Dutreaux," Vasco began, "there is something I must ask you—"

If it was about the Silver Cup I'd supposedly won, the masquerade was about to end. Vasco never finished.

At that instant the kitchen door opened, and Juapa walked through it, a bundle of mail under his arm.

Florita flushed and quickly began replacing the Sabatier cleavers into their slots on the preparation island. Juan's toothy idiot's grin slipped away. I felt Vasco tense. He fixed Juapa with a look that was plain. A kitchen was a chef's domain, and lo the stranger, who trod upon it with an uninvited step. Considering Juapa's temperament, Vasco's challenge took courage.

Juapa stopped short, and made that nervous click out of the side of his mouth. He beckoned to me. "The *patrón* wants you."

"At his convenience," I said, with no attempt to sound other than condescending.

"Now," said Juapa.

16

My apprehension began to rise the minute we'd left the kitchen. I wondered why Borrasa was so anxious to talk with Dutreaux. An informal word in the kitchen would have been adequate.

I followed Juapa through the double doors that led via a short hallway to a formal dining room. Beyond was a *sala*, done modern with lots of molded plywood, bright colors and overstuffed cushions, all arranged tastefully, but cold. A room you visit but don't really live in.

We went up a wide sweep of marble stairs to an interior balcony that overlooked the *sala*.

I didn't think I'd be as lucky finding the radio as I had the junction box in the larder, but I kept looking.

We walked past a row of plain white doors leading off the balcony; judging from their location, rooms looking out on the bay. One door was hasped and padlocked, the lock dangling loose and open.

The balcony made a ninety-degree turn, and so did we, stopping at the first door we came to. Next to it, through a low arch, I could see narrower stairs leading to another level. Juapa knocked once and, without waiting for an answer, opened the door, and we went in.

The library was enormous. An impression of chrome and white leather over a shiny terrazzo floor colored vanilla fudge.

Juapa tossed the bundle of mail onto a large semicircular desk done in Perspex and more chrome.

He flicked his chin toward the sliding glass doors at the end of the room.

"The *patrón* is there."

His mouth clicked. He was gone without a smile.

Behind me I heard one of the glass doors slide open, and a magnificent resonant voice say, "Welcome to the Villa Joyosa, Monsieur Dutreaux."

Luis Borrasa paused at the entrance as though it were the way he wanted you to remember him. At a distance he would have been many a woman's stranger across a crowded room. He was trim, dressed entirely in white. Deep tan, hair silvered. He looked exactly what he was. A man who had lost count of the zeros in his bankbook and had used a fair share of it on himself.

He walked quickly toward me, extending a hand. "The heat on the terrace is frightful." At a distance of five feet, the tan had a yellow tinge, the pouches showed beneath his eyes, and his face was all angles and deep lines. With his money, I didn't know what he had to look so worried about.

He stopped, squinting in the change of light. "I'd expected an older man." The idea made him pause before he smiled. "Drink?"

"In the heat of the day, never," I lied.

"Perrier, then?"

I said I would. He filled two tall glasses from makings on a small glass-topped table and handed one to me. He watched me steadily over the top of the glass.

"Your cable made no mention of my letter, Monsieur Dutreaux. You received it, I trust?" The question had a fragile quality.

I took longer with the first sip of Perrier than I had to.

There were a dozen reasons Borrasa might have written a letter to Claude Dutreaux. But only one reaction when Dutreaux received it. He'd want to know what was going on. He'd already been sacked. Whatever the subject of the letter, it would sound like jibberish.

"We took a brief holiday before coming on," I said. "I'm afraid not."

"How unfortunate. I thought you might find"—he

hesitated—"certain ingredients in Paris unobtainable here. No matter." His tone indicated it probably mattered very much. "I trust your accommodations are suitable?"

"Perfectly," I said. "The kitchen is more than adequate."

The lines around Borrasa's mouth curved into a lean smile.

"You French are seldom extravagant, with money or praise. The kitchen is magnificent and, you know it, unequaled in Spain." His arm made a sweep around the library. "Look around you, Dutreaux. Everything I own is unique. Possessing fine things is the only excuse one has for being rich. Power has uses, but I find it so abstract, don't you?"

He led me off around the room, first stopping at the desk. He rapped the Perspex top with his knuckles.

"A design by Aram. In our agreement I was assured he would never produce another like it." Borrasa poked at the bundle of mail Juapa had brought in and walked on.

My eyes stayed on the bundle. It was an inch or so thick, bound with a piece of rough brown string. The return address of the bottom letter stared up at me like a snake ready to strike. The address was in Paris' eighth *arrondissement*, a neighborhood I knew well. The name above the return address was simply, C. Dutreaux.

"The paintings of course all masterpieces," Borrasa said, pointing. "Donatello, there a Monet, and that early Picasso. You see I sympathize little with my government's formal censure of our exiled citizen. I find politics mundane. The senses, Dutreaux. And all things that impinge upon them. They are what is important to me."

I barely heard what he said. I was imagining all the things Dutreaux might have written in his letter to Borrasa. The fact that the letter existed at all after I'd already denied receiving his would peg me as a liar.

I had to get that letter.

I'd screwed up my courage enough to reach for it,

when Borrasa turned suddenly. "This, for example. Come closer, Dutreaux."

He beckoned me. From a table near the Picasso he picked up what appeared to be an ancient fencer's mask of dark, mottled ceramic. He turned it this way and that so I could see the details.

The mask was something out of an alcoholic's nightmare. Long devil's horns and little piggy eyes. Where the mouth should have been, the devil had something that looked like an ear trumpet extending a foot or so and turning upward.

"Magnificent," I said.

"Isn't it. A relic of the Inquisition. Put onto the faces of heretics, and here"—he pointed to the spout leading to the mouth—"was poured boiling oil. Note the eye holes. So that the inquisitors might search for repentance in the last seconds of agony. Torture, Dutreaux, the ultimate assault on the senses."

As I looked at the mask, the whole process was disconcertingly easy to visualize.

"The mask offends you?"

"It's a cruel way for anyone to die."

He smiled without warmth. "Until you know the Spanish, my friend, you know nothing of cruelty. Our women equal the men, I assure you." He laid the mask carefully on the table again. "I bought this particular piece from the Earl of Shrewsbury for a mere eight thousand pounds. Now come. I'll show you the prize. If I'm not boring you, Dutreaux?"

"I'm far from bored."

He led me through the sliding glass doors to the terrace. I'd thought for a moment he intended to show me the Frederika Diamond.

The terrace was about the size of a tennis court, with an oval swimming pool occupying a third of it. Borrasa walked directly to the brass telescope, swung it around on its gimbals, and pointed it down toward the beach.

He invited me to take a look.

My heart wasn't in it, my thoughts still on Dutreaux's letter. I twisted the eyepiece and brought the field into focus on the most beautiful woman I'd ever seen.

"My wife," Borrasa said behind me, his voice curiously empty.

Sylvia Borrasa lay beneath a dainty lace umbrella on the sand below. The black one-piece bathing suit clung like skin, emphasizing the kind of milky pale complexion that takes the sun slowly. Her features were fine, her nose straight and aristocratic, jet black hair stacked on her head in large, loose curls.

A pair of hands came into view and primped the hair. Sylvia Borrasa turned her classic face and said something I could tell was anything but ladylike. The pair of hands pulled back as though they'd touched hot metal. Vasco Ibarra's wife for a moment looked more frightened than sullen.

She hoisted her thick frame and scurried across the beach. I followed her until the sweep of telescope picked up something else. Sylvia was the prized item in Borrasa's collection, all right.

At the edge of the beach partially concealed in brush was a uniformed guard, the butt of a telescopic-sighted rifle planted firmly between his feet.

"Enough," said Borrasa. He led us back into the library. When he turned, the lines in his face had deepened.

"I sense, Monsieur Dutreaux, you are a man of some worldly experience. Your wife is a beautiful woman." He looked at me steadily. "A satisfied woman, no doubt."

I shrugged noncommittally. Borrasa was struggling to find words, speaking in a stilted formal French, rusty from disuse. I let him struggle. The conversation had taken a turn and was going off in a direction I didn't like.

He went on with some difficulty. "The señora and I have been married less than two months. I watched her mature from a child. Observed her beauty grow, I admit to you, with excitement." He paused and turned the bundle of letters on the desk, aimlessly. I couldn't watch. "She has led a sheltered life. She is shy." He looked up at me unhappily. "We as yet have not come to know one another fully."

He looked down at the bundle of mail and grew silent. I could feel perspiration on the back of my neck.

Borrasa cleared his throat. "I wrote to you in Paris hoping that in your repertoire there might be certain dishes. Sublime dishes." He paused. "Dishes to quicken the blood, if you understand me."

I understood him. A little grilled eel perhaps, a touch of powdered rhino horn in the olive oil. The Brits worry about their bowels, the French their liver. Latin men have an inordinate preoccupation with fresh water, corruption of their women, and paradoxically, maintenance of their manly powers by hook or crook. I'm a believer myself in the effect of a dozen Belon oysters, a bottle of icy Sancerre, and the right woman. If you have number three, you can forget about the rest. Whatever Borrasa's problem, he was desperate.

"It is not for me, understand."

"Of course."

"A young woman sometimes needs encouragement to take her place in God's order of things."

"I understand perfectly."

"I'd hoped before this time. . . ." He looked away, but his self-pity didn't last long. He straightened and said quickly, "My guests arrive tomorrow. Tonight will be our last of absolute solitude. I wish you to prepare dinner for two. Something appropriate, Dutreaux. To be served in the master bedroom by you yourself." I started to protest, but Borrasa raised a warning finger. "Now you may go."

He didn't even wait for my exit. He looked down at his desk, reached out, and snapped the string off the bundle of mail.

My heart began thumping in my chest, but I wasn't leaving without that letter. From where I stood my exit would take me in a straight line past the desk. If I could maneuver Borrasa away and distract him, even for a few seconds, I'd purloin Dutreaux's bloody missile and be home free.

I glanced around and saw absolutely nothing that might pull Borrasa's attention away from the desk and make him forget about me to boot. The only thing even in reach was that silly-looking devil's mask and I'd have had to throw it at him.

It was obvious then. That's exactly what I had to do.

I picked up the mask carefully. Any second Borrasa would look up. Then would come an angry demand to know what I was doing. I ought to be planning his *prélude d'amour*, not fondling his artifacts.

I looked at the proboscislike snout. I put the mask down again, balanced on the bottom edge of its face and the snout. It was off-balance and started to topple in a slow roll.

I propped it up near the edge of the table, balanced it, and let loose as I started for the door. Borrasa was still staring down.

I was almost even with the desk when behind me I heard a clunk, a hairsbreadth silence, then a crash as that horrible mask splattered itself all over the terrazzo floor.

Borrasa's eyes snapped up. When he pushed past me, I reached over the desk, snatched the bottom letter off the stack of mail, and stuck it into my pocket.

I spun around to face Borrasa, hoping my look was properly horrified. That was the easiest part of it. I'd already calculated how he would react to my clumsy disposal of his twenty-thousand-dollar antiquity. Borrasa was looking down at the pieces blankly.

"I must have bumped the table." My voice sounded hollow.

"So it would appear." He looked up and began to laugh.

I stared at him.

"You look as though you were expecting such a mask to be used on you, Dutreaux. Had it been real, perhaps."

"The mask wasn't genuine?"

"Of course not. All of this," he said, his arm sweeping

around the room, "is fake. Forgery of the best quality, naturally." He snorted, mocking. "Few people know the difference." He knocked on the wall at his back. "The originals are kept here. For my private pleasure."

"In a safe?"

"Of course in a safe. You seem surprised." He walked toward me, crushing the pieces of the phony mask beneath his feet, uncaring. "It is a vicious world, Dutreaux. Of prey, and those who are preyed upon. A man must guard his treasures cunningly." He smiled. "Don't you agree?"

17

"It can't be that bad, Sammy," said Davina.

I hadn't said anything to her until I'd found a bottle of sherry in the kitchen of the chef's quarters and poured some of it into a glass.

"I have one foot in a coffin and another on a banana peel, Davina. At this rate we'll be lucky to last out the day."

"Nonsense," she said, but she'd hesitated, unsure.

"Look, Dutreaux won a Silver Cup at Biarritz. To a chef it's the Nobel Prize and the Super Bowl rolled into one. I don't even know for what. Vasco started to question me in the kitchen, when Juapa came in."

"But Vasco is thrilled to death. You should have seen his face when he was talking to you."

"He's thrilled with Dutreaux, not me."

"Then you can't give him another reason to think you're not Dutreaux." Her eyes softened. "You can do it, Sammy."

"I haven't given you the big one yet." I told her about what happened in Borrasa's library. About the letter from the real Dutreaux and about Borrasa's demand that I prepare him and his reluctant bride a special dinner for two.

"What are you going to do?" She began to look worried.

"I don't know. Try an omelet with a few fine herbs maybe."

"Does that do anything?"

"It never has yet."

Davina rolled her eyes, her mouth going thin. "We'll have to think of something."

"Yes, we will." There was a moment of deadly silence. I was dragging Davina's spirit down with mine. "At least I found out a couple of things. The telephone junction box is in one of the kitchen larders. I haven't a clue to the radio yet, but one of the rooms along the balcony from Borrasa's library has a padlock."

"Why would they padlock their own radio?" Davina said disconsolately.

She had a point. "It might be on the top floor, then. There's a small stairway that leads up to rooms I haven't checked yet. Anyway, I found the safe."

"Big deal." Davina put her chin on her hands.

"It's in the library, behind the wall with the Picasso on it."

"Caleb said it would be in the library."

It took a moment before her remark sank in. "Not to me, he didn't. Howard and Caleb made a big point of how much trouble you'd have finding the safe."

Davina looked up. "I only meant Caleb had a hunch."

"Davina. . . ."

"I'm sorry I mentioned it." She stood up quickly and started for the other room.

I caught her arm and pulled her around. "I knew it didn't ring right. Even Coudert smelled it. Knowing everything, right down to the make of safe, but not knowing where it was."

"Let go of my goddamn arm."

"Sit down." I pushed her into a chair. She looked at me, surprised. "If finding that safe was no big deal, exactly why are you here?" Her eyes moved away. "There's more to this raid, isn't there, Davina?"

She made a careless shrug. "I have a special job, Sammy, that's all. Nothing to do with the diamond or what Howard told you and Coudert."

"Why did he keep it a secret?"

"For your own good."

I sighed. "Davina, do you know how many lives have

been ruined by people doing things to other people for their own bloody good?"

"Howard thought the less you knew, the better. In case you were caught and they did something to you. You can't blab what you don't know."

"Well, thanks for the confidence."

I felt the anger rising, when we both heard it. A quiet but insistent tapping at the front door of the chef's quarters.

There was a frozen moment until I realized if it was Juapa after my hide, it would have been more than tap, tap, tap.

I went to the door and looked through the Judas hole. It was Vasco Ibarra. I opened the door, a crack.

"*Mil perdones*, Chef Dutreaux."

"We are resting, Chef Ibarra. The trip was tiring."

"I'm sorry that I must disturb you. It is a matter of some urgency." He didn't move. A piece of paper twisted nervously in his pudgy hands.

I wasn't about to risk adding insult to whatever doubts Vasco may have had at that moment about Dutreaux's competence. Spaniards are so bloody sensitive.

"I am at your service."

"It is about the banquet, Chef Dutreaux." His eyes looked a little sadder.

"What banquet?"

"I thought the *patrón* would have mentioned it to you."

"We talked of other things."

"Naturally. It is of slender importance," he said, bobbing his head politely. "But it is tomorrow night."

I opened the door wider. "Maybe you'd better come in."

"A formal banquet," Vasco was saying. "The traditional welcome to the house of Borrasa."

"How many people?"

"A mere eight."

It might as well have been eighty. "I see." I plopped

into a chair. Davina eased into the room, working on her nails again, following every word.

"Of course I have arranged everything," said Vasco. He smiled humbly. "On such short notice I knew you would not possibly undertake a banquet."

"I wouldn't deprive you of the honor, in any case. Consider me but an adviser, a friend in the kitchen."

"You are most gracious, Chef Dutreaux. For it is in this matter I have come to you." Vasco unrolled the piece of paper. "The menu for the banquet. I would value your opinion."

Davina stopped filing and stared down at her nails.

Intentional or not, it was an open challenge. Fail him and Vasco would have more than a fleeting suspicion that Dutreaux wasn't the man he was supposed to be.

I took the piece of paper and had a look. I suppose there had been menus to equal it, one of Escoffier's minor dos at the old Petit-Moulin Rouge maybe. Eight courses began with Astrakhan caviar and crepes Moscovites, followed by velouté Marie Stuart and suprême de sole au champagne. The baron d'agneau de Pauillac would arrive with petits pois, haricots verts and pommes Anna. Those who could go on would have crayfish, asparagus and foie gras. The wines were all Premier Grand Cru Classe in years I'd only heard about. The brandy was a fine old pre-World War I Hine which Papa Victor said was as good as this century had produced. The cigars were Cuban. It was a beautiful menu, a work of art really, created about half a century too late.

Vasco looked anxious. "It is somehow . . . lacking. Perhaps champagne." He stopped, watched me, and waited.

His mention of champagne reminded me of something, and I had to get back on the offense.

I shook my head. "Lacking, no," I said. "Excess. An unfortunate habit of the Spanish."

I saw Davina stiffen. Vasco looked as though he'd taken a shot between the eyes. "I don't understand."

"Then you must. Knowing food is not enough, Chef Ibarra. One must understand eating as well. The stomachs of the rich, my friend, are no bigger than yours or mine."

I was on my feet then, talking as I paced.

"But the dishes . . ." he began. Vasco looked dazed.

I couldn't let him get started. "Are magnificent. Each one a masterpiece."

His head bobbed, uncertainly. "There is still much to learn."

"But together. . . ." I made a spiraling, throwaway gesture with my right hand I'd seen Papa Victor do a hundred times.

Vasco went pale. Davina was working the nail file like a chain saw. I bent toward him. "A meal is a symphony, Chef Ibarra. The courses, movements building toward the ultimate crescendo." His eyes became thoughtful. "But there must always be counterpoint, a change of tempo to keep the palate alive. Too much fortissimo and the palate will never recover."

"Yes," said Vasco slowly. "Yes."

"And the themes, restated here, underplayed there." I waved the menu at him. "Too many themes, Chef Ibarra. Too much fortissimo."

Vasco looked dumbstruck. "I have never understood it so clearly."

But I was running on, trying to remember the clincher. "And when you finish a menu, there is always one thing still to do."

He leaned toward me. Fire was behind those sad brown eyes. "Yes, Chef Dutreaux. . . ."

"Simplify."

"Simplify?" He seemed a bit let-down. "But how does one simplify a great symphony?"

I plopped into the chair again. I'd stretched it to the limit. "One isn't taught such things, Chef Ibarra. One must learn them. The menu is in your hands."

Perspiration glistened on Vasco's forehead. "I won't fail your trust."

"Now, if you'll excuse us. The señora and I need rest."

"Is there something I can do?"

I started to decline, then had an idea. "I couldn't trouble you, Chef Ibarra."

"No trouble would be too great."

"A simple meal for two. Something light, to revive a tired spirit."

"I have just the thing. A magnificent Féra received chilled this morning."

Féra is a very fine Lake Geneva salmon. Old impotent Alden from Walden, ate salmon to heat him to scaldin'. "With perhaps a caper sauce," I said, "and a modest champagne, well iced." Davina was looking at me as though I'd lost a few washers. "We'll dine here."

Vasco gave me a shy smile. When he'd left, I found the bottle of Tio Pepe again, poured a water glass to the brim, and drank it.

Davina followed me into the bedroom. She slipped out of her dress, popped off her bra, and stood fanning herself with a copy of *La Moda*. Even with my mind on other things, Davina's breasts were distracting.

"You're amazing, Sammy. I really mean it."

"I'm amazing all right."

"Vasco left here thinking you're the greatest thing since peanut butter."

"Be happy he came to ask about a menu and not Dutreaux's Silver Cup. We were lucky."

"That symphony speech was fantastic."

"I thought so too, the first time I heard it. From an Austrian chef named Winkel at Searcy's, sick of weddings and banquets. Got tipsy on the Bollinger's and gave that same speech to the whole kitchen. I remember things like that. I'm great with other people's words."

"Why are you so sore?"

"Because I have nothing of my own, Davina. No-thing. You know what that means to a person?"

"You're a born con, Sammy. You haven't realized it yet, that's all. Caleb says the same thing."

"He does, does he?"

"Says if he had a face like yours, he'd still be playing poker."

"Caleb said that?"

She nodded. "What you're doing, none of us could get away with. We all know it."

I shook my head. "I don't know how much longer I can make it work."

"It's going to be all right." She came close to me and began unbuttoning my shirt. "You need something to take your mind off things, Sammy."

"A trip to Copenhagen."

"You'll like this even better." She led me toward the bed. "I promise."

Vasco brought dinner just after nine. I'd hoisted myself weakly out of bed a few minutes before, letting Davina sleep. Presuming we survived that long, there wouldn't be much of it the next night.

Vasco brought in the tray with a tight expression I recognized as one chef's concern over how another would accept his efforts. Davina was right in one respect. If Vasco had wavered in his acceptance of Dutreaux, any question had gone. Vasco's allegiance was mine.

The tray was nicely done. With the salmon he'd added two asparagus cocktails of the big-headed, white variety the Spanish consider such a delicacy.

Arranged as they were, the asparagus peeking over the top of their cups reminded me of those smutty cartoons we used to pass around in grade school titled "Bride's Nightmare" or some such. I hoped for Borrasa's sake it wasn't too obvious.

I lifted the lid on the salmon, sniffed the caper sauce, felt the chill on the champagne, and pronounced it adequate.

"You are most kind, Chef Dutreaux," Vasco cooed. When he'd left, I changed into fresh kitchen whites, shouldered the tray and made my way to the second floor of the villa, avoiding the kitchen.

The master bedroom was between Borrasa's library

and the door off the balcony with the hasp and padlock.

I stopped outside the door and listened. From inside came the unmistakable staccato of a Spanish woman in the midst of an angry harangue. Sylvia Borrasa was having at her new husband; the tone of it reminded me of old Señora Muñoz lowering the boom on Caleb. The same Andalusian accent was unmistakable.

I knocked quietly, heard the voice stop, and nodded when Borrasa opened the door, his face taut with strain.

It took me less than a minute. I laid out a spread for two on a small circular table near the window, lit candles, and sprung the cork on the champagne, filling two glasses.

Out of the corner of my eye I saw Borrasa pacing, his hands gripped tightly behind his back with impatience.

Sylvia Borrasa watched me impassively, the directness of her gaze broken only by the occasional flutter of long dark lashes. She was meant for champagne and candlelight, her perfect oval face looking as though it were carved from fine pale ivory.

I felt a moment's sympathy with Borrasa; I wouldn't have known how to handle her either.

When I'd finished, Borrasa gave me a curt wave of dismissal. "If I want you, I'll ring."

At the door I turned and gave a courteous bow. Borrasa had already turned his back, extending his hand to Sylvia. I know he missed what happened next. In the half-light I wasn't sure I saw it myself.

As Sylvia Borrasa stood, offering him her hand as though bestowing a great favor, she glanced sideways toward me.

One of those large eyes blinked, a long, lewd wink.

18

Borrasa's banquet began a little past ten the next evening. The day preceding it was the longest of my life.

Before I was fully awake, Davina was out of bed, dressed, and heading for the door. I raced her for it, naked, and didn't quite make it. From outside, she waved aside my demand to tell me what she was up to in a matter-of-fact way worthy of Howard.

"Not now, Sammy. I have things to do." She was dressed in a trim black uniform, with a plain white apron. She looked surprisingly well in it.

I spent most of the day sitting in the toilet with the door closed, avoiding everyone. Nothing good would come of a chance meeting with Juapa or Borrasa. As it was, I'd have to appear in the kitchen during the banquet or risk offending Vasco.

Sylvia's enigmatic wink the night before and the fact that I still hadn't a clue to the location of the radio gnawed at me like a pair of hungry rats.

It was early evening before Davina returned. I'd already shaved, bathed very slowly, and was dressing in fresh kitchen whites when she came in, sighed, and toed off her shoes.

"Well, that's over." She dropped into a chair.

I folded the kerchief, looped it around my neck, and knotted it without saying anything.

"I found out which guest villas will be occupied by who. Then had that greaseball Juapa take me into La Boca, when he picked up Girondas and his wife. Now there's a sexy man. Yummy and animal. I left the note for Howard at the Hotel Luz."

I tried on the chef's toque and looked at myself in the mirror.

"Howard gave me something for you," Davina said, frowning at my silence.

It was a note. It said only: "Take heart. Tomorrow. . . ." Followed by a long row of dollar signs.

"Very funny."

"I know something else you'll think is funny. I saw Borrasa."

She slipped the zipper down on her uniform, stepped out of it and everything else and walked into the bathroom. "He was meeting his guests at the boathouse, with a very long face." She began filling the tub. "I'd avoid him if I were you."

"I haven't been out. I didn't find the radio, either."

"It's in a room on the top floor. The other room up there is Juapa's bedroom, so be careful."

"How do you know?"

Davina peered around the doorway. "I didn't find out the way you think I found out. I had Florita take me on a tour, and I looked. Sammy, you're not still sore because I haven't told you every teensy thing?"

"Sore? I'm bloody raw."

Splashing sounds came from the tub. "Don't be silly, darling. You're the only one we're all depending on." She began humming "Michele."

I pulled the toque off my head and threw it against the wall. Even without Davina's help I felt wrong and looked wrong.

I dug around in my suitcase until I found the silk bag yellowed with age. From it I took Papa Victor's velvet beret. It had a long black tassel in the center. Worn in the kitchen, it was the kind of vanity only the very best chefs are allowed, and I felt mean and guilty when I put it on. It was undeniably the right touch.

Davina came out of the bathroom working the towel across her body. "Ummm. You look nice."

"I don't deserve to wear this."

"Don't be a nit. You're gorgeous." She let the towel fall away and wrapped her arms around me.

"You'll leave blotches."

"At the farmhouse, Sammy. And since we've been here. Don't you feel if we had enough time it could keep getting better and better? You and me, I mean."

"Howard and Caleb could never take the pain of having you gone."

She looked thoughtful, maybe a little too much so. "Things get complicated, don't they, Sammy?"

"Only after the age of ten." I untangled her arms, tilted the beret at a rakish angle, and walked down the path to the kitchen, mad at everyone, myself at the top of the list.

The start of the raid was seven hours away.

I was still mad when I walked into the kitchen. I've found a little bad temper sometimes brings out the best in other people, for some perverse reason. Or perhaps it was Papa Victor's beret.

I stopped in the doorway, breathed in that fantastic mixture of aromas, and gave just the slightest nod of approval.

When Vasco saw me, his moves took on an unmistakable new authority, and the staff seemed to stand straighter.

The vegetable girl, Florita, blushed, and old Juan grinned, before he scooped away the clutter from the preparation table as though garbage were fun.

I had an involuntary rush of pride for my *brigade de cuisine* and allowed myself just the smallest strut around the kitchen, praying nobody asked me to do anything.

It took only one tour to see Vasco had beautifully simplified the menu to four courses built around crayfish and the baron of lamb. In a corner of the kitchen were a dozen magnums of Perrier-Jouet '59, their lovely long necks peering up from shaved ice.

At the final moment Vasco rushed up and asked me to cast the last critical eye on his work as it left the kitchen. "Please, Chef Dutreaux," he said warmly. "I would consider it an honor."

"As would I, Chef Ibarra."

The service of the banquet was smooth and unobtrusive, a minor coup of timing itself. From my position in the hall just outside the dining room I could see enough of Borrasa's guests to tell they considered excellence their due.

They'd all been beautiful people once, but with the exception of Sylvia Borrasa it had gone stale long ago.

At the head of the table Borrasa was tanned and smooth and smiling. Except, when attention turned elsewhere, his face lapsed into a frown.

He turned and said something to the guest at his left, a pale cadaver of a man with almost transparent skin, and large spatulate hands. The cadaver followed conversation around the table with alert eyes, but spoke seldom and smiled not at all. Schiller, the Swiss banker, without doubt.

Next to him, Señora Schiller was distinguished plainly by the diamond and emerald tiara that winked from atop her elaborately coiffed head. She was sleek and laquered, but her noble Colombian ancestry and fine features were going slack, I suspected from never having had to lift a finger. Her neck probably hurt from holding up the tiara.

She laughed, openmouthed, when the dark, round man next to her, with even darker feminine eyes, whispered something close to her ear and patted her hand with a small hairy hand of his own. Mahmoud Falek wasn't at ease. Venturing among that crowd hoping to raise money must have been like walking on eggs.

He added a forced laugh and turned as if to pass on the idea to the woman at his left.

Next to him Leila Falek responded dutifully with a shrill squeal. The way she was sitting I couldn't see those famous hips. From the look of her I imagined a few years before I might have got a squint cheap in one of Falek's brothels.

Duty done, she promptly forgot her husband's existence, which is just like an ex-hooker, and smiled at the man across from her.

She would have needed newer equipment than she had. Nikolides Girondas hunched over his plate, his short, powerful frame dominating one side of the table, his almost sensuous mouth working at the serious business of chewing.

He stared straight through Leila Falek, grunting periodically, but his eyes said it all. Girondas had savored too many pleasures in his life; eating was one of the few he continued to enjoy. He was bored.

Next to him Mrs. Girondas smiled distantly, her pleasant peasant's face resigned to Lord knew how many years of her beloved Niko's inattention. She had the look of a homebody; she'd probably have enjoyed herself more in the kitchen.

It was impossible not to stare at Sylvia Borrasa. Her youth and beauty next to the rest of them were an arrogant display. She was also a spoiled brat. She wasn't even trying. She stared sullenly at her plate, picking at her food, and made Borrasa sweat for every word.

If it hadn't been for the magnificent Frederika Diamond rolling across the cleavage between pale breasts to remind me, I'd have wondered why she'd married Borrasa in the first place.

I forced my eyes away from the diamond and looked carefully into the shadows around the edges of the dining room. No sign of Juapa or the three armed guards.

By my watch the raid began in less than five hours.

With the final course on the table, Vasco was there next to me, peering through the crack in the door into the dining room.

"They ate well, Chef Dutreaux." There was satisfaction in his voice.

"A greater tribute a chef could not ask."

My eyes were back again on Sylvia and the diamond. I'd been watching the way she toyed with it, carelessly. As though it were nothing more to her than a trinket. Borrasa's remark in the library about guarding one's treasures suddenly separated itself from the murk in the back of my mind. I'd nearly missed it.

"A diamond worthy of a beautiful woman," I said.

"They are of equal value." The irony was clear in his voice.

With Vasco's wife attending young Sylvia, Vasco was likely to share any secret worth knowing.

"You don't approve of the new señora?"

"It is not for me to approve or disapprove, Chef Dutreaux. The women of the Sierra are not always trustworthy."

"They are man and wife."

"Under the law."

"And she wears the diamond. Surely an indication of his trust?"

"Perhaps." The silence was pregnant.

"A copy?" said I, amazed.

Vasco touched his lips with a finger.

"Chef Ibarra, the secret is safe with me."

After the coffee they followed the inviolate Latin custom and separated into two groups. The women retreated to the *sala*, while Borrasa led the gentlemen upstairs to the library for brandy and cigars.

The question was how long the men's session would last. I glanced at my watch. It was already 2 A.M.

I insisted that Vasco retire. I, Dutreaux, would close the kitchen. Vasco got that watery look I'd seen on the patio that first day. He couldn't contain himself. He rushed forward and gave me a parting embrace. "We will do great things, eh?"

I told him we would.

While I waited for old Juan to work his way through the pots and pans, I opened a bottle of champagne.

Florita lingered over some tasks in the pantry until she realized I intended to be the last out of the kitchen. Then she smiled an angelic smile, curtsied, and left.

Old Juan took a long time putting a final edge on the knives and cleavers. He returned them carefully to their separate slots. When he was done, he looked up and grinned an idiotic but satisfied smile. Maybe Juan had the secret, after all.

By the time he was gone, it was after three. I had a look around, saw everything was scrubbed and clean. I took the bottle with me and left.

Davina was still up, pacing nervously. "For chrissakes, where have you been?"

"Shepherding my flock."

"We haven't much time."

I began changing my clothes. "What do you mean, we?"

"I mean you." She looked at the bottle. "You haven't been drinking?"

"You don't sound sure."

"Sammy . . ." she growled.

"You didn't think I'd do this sober?"

She walked around in a tight circle, talking up at the ceiling. "Honest, if I knew what made me go for the men I do, I'd have it cut out."

I stopped dressing. "You mean me?"

"What do you think I've been trying to tell you?"

"Why didn't you just say it?"

"Would it have made a difference?" She looked away. "You wouldn't have believed me. You'd have thought it was part of Howard's plan."

"Let's talk about it."

"Not now."

"When?"

"When this is over." She looked at me, exasperated. "Sammy, go!"

I examined myself in the mirror. Cary Grant I was, dressed entirely in black. Robie the Cat ready to dance across the rooftops.

I opened the suitcase, fished out Caleb's alarm clock bomb, a Swiss Army knife, and the two plastic envelopes filled with gray gunk for the radio.

"Go!" Davina hissed.

"You don't think we ought to synchronize our watches?"

I didn't wait for an answer.

I took another drink of champagne and slipped out into the night.

19

I went down the path to the kitchen for the second and I hoped last time that night. It was steep and uneven, and I moved slowly to keep from going flat on my face.

I'd left a single light on in the kitchen as a beacon. The night hadn't a hint that dawn was less than an hour away.

I'd already decided the thermite bomb in the telephone junction box had first priority. It had a timing device, and I planned to be long gone when it went off.

I let myself into the kitchen and went across to the double doors leading to the rest of the villa. The men were still at their brandy apparently; a vague rumble of voices sounded elsewhere in the villa.

I went straight to the larder then, leaving the door open wide enough to allow a ray of light from the kitchen to fall squarely on the gray metal junction box.

I used the screwdriver blade on the Swiss Army knife to remove the two screws that held the cover in place and lifted it aside.

Inside, several bundles of color-coded wires fed off both sides of a central terminal block. The symmetry of it made me hesitate, and I shouldn't have.

It would have taken more champagne than I'd had to forget the truth of it. I was about to commit the first overt act. Everything up to this point had been on paper and subject to possible explanation. It was Begay who was about to set the process in motion. I shook the idea off and told myself that the raid was in fact already in progress. By this time Coudert and his men had been ashore two hours, and Howard and Caleb were out there somewhere waiting for the fireworks to begin. Any hesitation on my part now would only diminish the chances for success.

My palms began to sweat. Around me was the sickly sweet smell of chorizo and the unmistakable aroma of dried cod.

I took the small alarm clock, set it to the correct time, and wound it tightly. The alarm pointer had been preset so the thermite would discharge exactly nineteen minutes before Caleb blew up the launch and Coudert started to work with his machine guns.

I double checked the settings, listened for the tick, and pulled out the alarm plunger making it operative.

I put the alarm into the junction box and replaced the cover.

I stood up, vowing I'd never eat chorizo again from the association. I'd taken one step toward the larder door, when every nerve in my body went gyppo.

Someone was standing in the kitchen.

For a minute I wasn't even sure how I knew. I listened and heard nothing. For once I let my instinct overrule my brain, which kept saying hopefully, "Don't be silly, Sammy, there is absolutely no reason for anyone to be in the kitchen. Get a move on."

I remained perfectly still.

Then I heard it again. The nervous click Juapa made out of the side of his mouth.

My first reaction was instinctive. Juapa had no right to be in the kitchen. Outrage at that moment wouldn't have done me a bit of good. I was standing two feet inside the larder, almost completely lit by the slice of kitchen light. I was dressed in black. I'd just put a thermite bomb in the phone system and had two other parcels that weren't, as far as I knew, edible.

I looked out into the wedge of kitchen and held my breath. A match flared, and Juapa walked into view not four feet away. He took a deep drag on his cigarette, his profile toward me. If he turned ninety degrees in my direction and glanced through the larder door, he'd see a sweaty, familiar face screwed up the size of a dime.

I remained perfectly still. So did Juapa. For what seemed an eternity.

Then he began a slow circuit of the kitchen, disappearing from my field of view. I was beginning to worry we'd both be in exactly the same place when the thermite bomb went off. I didn't stand a hope of removing it from the junction box without noise. Juapa seemed content, in a restless sort of way, to spend the early-morning hours wandering around the kitchen.

Then I heard the outside door open and click shut.

Florita came into the kitchen, with a look on her face that didn't need words to translate. My angelic Florita.

She looked at Juapa, moaned passionately, and lunged for him. Second surprise. Juapa returned her embrace with a hunger of his own. I knew what was about to happen then. I had no choice but to observe.

I have a kind of memory that accumulates facts and bits of other people's ideas and just as promptly forgets the source. Papa Victor was the same way. At that point I remembered reading somewhere that man is one of the few animals that chooses to copulate front to front. Along with the pygmy chimpanzee, the porcupine, the hamster, and the two-toed sloth. Waiting there, watching Juapa and Florita, it was difficult to believe man was anything but an animal, after all, and one that takes very seriously what ought to be a lot of fun.

The other thing I thought of was that they were undoubtedly a pair of Europeans, not from the fact that the special words they were using had no meaning to me whatsoever, but because he shaved beneath his arms and she didn't.

I don't know how long it went on. It seemed like a long time. When things reached the inevitable dénouement and the racket died away, neither of them lingered.

Juapa slipped past the door of the larder, smoothing his feathers. He went out the double door to the dining room. A second later Florita left the way she'd come. And not so much as a *buenas noches* between them.

I forced myself to wait another five minutes, then went through the dining room and the *sala*.

I had to move now.

The rest of it turned out easier than I expected. I went straight up the marble stairs and along the inside balcony, past Borrasa's library.

I could hear voices inside, and it would have been awkward if someone had decided to leave at that moment. Nobody did.

I went through the arch and up the small stairway to the top floor of the villa. Davina's reconnaissance had been accurate. There were only two doors. I listened at one and heard nothing. From behind the other came a low static hum. I took a deep breath and went in.

An orange light glowed on a piece of apparatus with "Marconi" lettered across the face in metal script. There were three or four other boxes I didn't bother to study.

I took the plastic envelopes, squeezed the glass ampules, and placed them according to Caleb's instructions. Then I went home.

The magnum of champagne was where I'd left it, on the living-room table. It still had a chill. I looked at my watch and found I'd been gone less than half an hour.

I took a sip of champagne and undressed in the living room so I wouldn't disturb Davina. My physical energy had been tapped down to zero, but I had a peculiar elation. I'd done my job. There was nothing to do now but wait. I found myself just the wee bit perturbed that Davina had folded up and gone to bed while I'd been out risking life and limb for the success of this bloody venture.

I drank more champagne and went into the bedroom. She was in bed, the sheet pulled up. The room was dark and cool, and bed with Davina was the only place I wanted to be. The thought was rather a surprise.

I slipped in next to her and gave her buttock a pat. She'd gone to bed angrier with me than I'd thought, fully dressed, which wasn't her way. It irritated me. There are times when one appreciates a little skin.

"Davina." I gave her a shake.

"Shhh."

"I will not shhhh. I'm back."

I was greeted with silence.

Welcome the bloody hero. I sat up, flipped on the light, and pulled her around.

Davina turned over, sat up, and stared at me with a pair of hard black eyes. Except it wasn't Davina.

I was looking into the beautiful, angry face of Sylvia Borrasa.

20

One of us might have screamed if someone hadn't started pounding at the door.

I went for the living room. However I was to be caught with Sylvia Borrasa, it wasn't going to be in bed or even with my clothes off.

When the pounding changed to a series of violent kicks, I had a hunch who was working over the front door. The moulding around the latch splintered and started to come away.

I had on trousers, shirt, and shoes without socks when Juapa burst through the door like that scene in *The Thing*. He stood glaring, a heavy pistol pointing around the room with a bore the size of a railway tunnel.

"Here now," I said, advancing, putting my faith in outrage.

He waited until I was in arm's reach, then, without hesitating, backhanded me with the pistol. A yellow flash and I was on the floor, my right shoulder numb to my neck.

The room tilted, and I thought for a moment Juapa had slid out through the open door. I was almost on my feet again when he came into the living room from the bedroom and pointed the gun at me.

"Where is the woman?"

"What woman?" I made a bad try at sounding a very wronged Dutreaux; the slap with the pistol had taken it out of me for pretending.

Juapa grinned, nastily. "The one who says she's your wife."

I had one fleeting moment of thankfulness that Sylvia Borrasa had managed to remove herself from my bed. I didn't have time to worry about Davina.

Juapa jerked me to my feet and shoved me ahead of him out the door. The pain was settling into nausea.

He prodded me down the path toward the Villa Joyosa, his hand hooked in the back of my trousers so I couldn't run. I glanced up, noticing the barest thread of pink stretched across the horizon, and promptly slipped on the gravel paving.

I went over like a bowling pin, taking Juapa with me. I heard a pained grunt, and the clatter of metal as the pistol skittered away across gravel.

I was already up and running. I plunged ahead down the path and into the kitchen with no plan except away. I thought of going through the villa to the boathouse, then along the beach. The idea lasted as far as the door that led from the kitchen to the dining room. Someone had locked it.

Behind me the kitchen light went on with a loud click.

Juapa was standing in the doorway, shirt filthy, his linen trousers torn at the knee. The look on his face said no one did that to Juapa.

Very deliberately he took a long spring knife from his pocket and held it up so I could see. The blade sprang open with an appropriately threatening metallic snap. Juapa looked at me and laughed.

There must be some conditioning factor in learning to confront danger. Juapa with his pistol had frozen me into near immobility. But standing where he was, brandishing a knife, it was an entirely different thing.

There is nothing the least bit intimidating to me about someone waving a sharp blade in a kitchen, even in anger. I once saw a Filipino salad chef stab the maître d'hôtel in the kitchen of the Cumberland over an affair of honor involving a tainted salade japonaise. A chef I knew at the Carlton once took off a thumb joint while boning a chicken leg for the chicken surprise and told me he'd be bleeding still if the pastry cook hadn't reacted quickly with a tin of sifted flour. A wielded knife accompanied by the crunch of bone and sight of blood are as common in a kitchen as in an operating theater. Juapa may have made a minor miscalculation. He had chosen to do away with me in my own arena.

His mouth made that nervous click, and he came toward me along one side of the preparation island.

I backed around, keeping it between us. If we continued that way, I'd simply keep in front of him until I had a shot at the back door. How many minutes or seconds we had before the thermite bomb in the larder went off, I hadn't a guess.

Juapa stopped, backtracked, slightly puzzled I wasn't showing more signs of panic.

He made a slashing motion with the knife and told me what he planned to cut off first.

We started a little dance then, Juapa feinting this way and moving that, me doing my best to keep the preparation island between us. Then he made a rush.

I slid off around the island ahead of him, my hand brushing the handle of the Sabatier cleaver. I seized on it like a familiar friend. I slowed a step, then pivoted, in the same motion swinging the cleaver around in a wide arc. I missed spilling Juapa's innards by a clear foot, but it stopped him short just the same.

He stood his ground and dropped into a crouch, the knife held low.

To my left, a large tin of those plump skinless tomatoes Spanish chefs would be lost without was within arm's reach. It was impulse based probably on the realization that I wouldn't really win any contest of knives with Juapa.

In a quick overarm movement with lots of wrist snap in it I reached out with the cleaver and split the tin down the middle.

There was an ominous sound of metal cleanly shearing metal, a second when nothing appeared to have happened, before the two sides of the tin separated and those red tomatoes came spilling out all over the place.

I looked at Juapa across the mess. His eyes, riveted on the ooze, had just the slightest flash of uncertainty.

I didn't wait for any more advantages. I gave a good mock-karate yell and with my left hand swept off the entire layer of pots and pans from the top of the preparation island. They hit the floor, tumbling. I reared back and winged the cleaver toward Juapa. He jumped agilely sidewise, put his foot on a ten-liter casserole, and went down. He called me a lover of goats and scrambled up, but not before I was past him and out the kitchen door, running along the back of the villa, going I knew not where.

I turned the corner of the villa and started down toward the boathouse and the beach. I'd covered about half the distance when a shadow came around the corner of the villa below me.

A torch beam caught me full in the face. "There," a voice said in Spanish, and the shadow, joined by two others, came running up the hill toward me.

My legs wouldn't have carried me back in the direction I'd come even without the likelihood Juapa was somewhere behind me. I dropped into a crouch, expecting gunfire, and darted at right angles to the house, moving along the slope of the hill. The torch beam stayed with me a few seconds, then inexplicably went out.

I went a good hundred yards before I stopped. The ground was rocky and covered with low thorny scrub, not thick enough to hide in but sharp enough to jab me everywhere from the thighs down. My shoes were filled with gravel, reminding me I'd forgotten to put on socks. But unless the people behind me had followed on little cat feet, I'd made good my escape. I looked back; great slabs of light were going on in the Villa Joyosa.

As much as my body would have approved, I knew I couldn't stay where I was. My break away from the Villa Joyosa had been parallel and above the stone road that ringed the perimeter of the bay. I was above the first of the guest villas.

I looked down at my watch. The crystal had shattered, stopping it at four thirty. Whatever else happened it would be light soon. In which case Juapa and his men would be able to pick me off the hillside like a cherry. Also, by my reckoning, I was at that moment smack in the middle of the area due to be swept by Coudert's machine guns.

It took me five minutes to grapple straight up the hill on all fours. Then another five to move at right angles toward the chef's quarters.

On the way to the boathouse and the villa Howard and Caleb would have to pass very close. Howard's orders had been to stay put until the raid was over and he'd come for us.

I wondered then what had become of Davina, then decided it was effort better spent on myself. In typical Williamson fashion, she avoided trouble completely. The thought of Sylvia Borrasa in my bed and Juapa knowing somehow of the Dutreaux deception made her disappearance suspiciously well timed.

When I reached the chef's quarters, I climbed the hill still farther, content to wait in the darkness until whatever came next was over.

I didn't wait long. My only warning was the barest scrape of shoe against stone. I'd half turned toward the sound when the blow struck. I was still partially conscious and tried to turn away and stand at the same time. I thought later the force of the blow had affected my vision.

I could think of no other reason why I should have thought it was Howard standing over me, his arm poised an instant before it came down again on my head.

21

"Come along, my dear Begay," a voice was saying sweetly.

I would have gone anywhere with that friendly voice, except I was filled with lead. There had been a while when I'd felt weightless, floating over a great dark landscape. But I'd come to earth again, and someone had hollowed out my body from eyelids to toes and filled it with birdshot.

"Come now, Begay," sweet voice said. Then the voice changed. "We can't waste any more time. Wake him."

Someone pried open my mouth and forced brandy into it. I choked myself upright and looked straight into the face of Juapa.

Borrasa watched me dispassionately over his shoulder. "Careful he doesn't bleed on the leather," he said.

I was in Borrasa's library. A smoky oppressiveness hung in the air like an all-night pool hall.

I moved my head around and found my neck fused rigid. To move hurt even my eyeballs. I tried once, saw a clock that said five straight up, and wondered whether it was night or day. I decided to stop torturing myself and started to shut my eyes. Juapa reached out and slapped me sharply across the mouth.

"Too much of that already," said Borrasa. He edged in front of Juapa and bent toward me. "I want the details, Señor Begay." This time when he used my name it struck home. "Ah, yes, your deception is no more."

He waved a passport at me, my own. I'd left it behind, with my other things, at the farmhouse with Howard.

"How did I get here?"

"You availed yourself by collapsing on my doorstep. No matter. Now I want to know everything."

"I don't know anything."

A low growl came from Juapa, and he started to close in.

Borrasa restrained him with an outstretched hand. "Please, Señor Begay. I dislike hurting you needlessly, despite your rude joke with me. But there is a certain urgency. We already know a great deal."

He turned and pointed to the table behind him. On it was the tiny Swiss alarm clock I'd put in the telephone junction box.

"We also found packages of chemicals with the radio."

"I wanted to be alone."

He straightened up and nodded to Juapa. "Use the pool. Quickly now."

Juapa jerked me upright and out onto the terrace. He pulled an ornate wrought-iron garden chair to the edge of the swimming pool and pushed me into it. He began tying me with a length of wire clothesline, and when I realized what they intended to do, I tried to fight him.

He stepped back long enough to hit me squarely in the face, and I lost track for a few seconds. The next thing I knew I was tied securely in the chair and tottering on the edge of the pool, restrained only by the end of the length of clothesline Juapa held in his hand.

He glanced toward Borrasa.

"Last chance, Señor Begay. We'll find out sooner or later. It would be easier if it were sooner."

"Victim of circumstance." I was having trouble with words.

Juapa didn't even wait for a signal. He gave the line slack and let me and the iron chair drop off into the deep end of the swimming pool. I had just enough presence to grab a big breath of air, before we went straight to the bottom.

The admirable thing about Howard and Caleb was their almost unfailing understanding of human nature, their ability to anticipate what people might do and to make plans accordingly. They'd pegged my ability to endure interrogation to a T. When Juapa had started punching me around, I'd made the stubborn decision at some lower level of consciousness that I wasn't going to give Borrasa or Juapa a thing. It wasn't out of any allegiance to Howard or Caleb or even Davina. I had more than a creeping suspicion what their intentions were. It was allegiance to myself, and it was worth taking a beating for.

The trouble is everyone has elemental fears. Of spiders or snakes or of harm to one's family. The effective interrogator need only find out which of those is applicable to be instantly effective. Mine is of being smothered. Of somehow not being able to expand my chest and fill my lungs with air. To drown is to smother in the worst possible way. Juapa left me on the bottom of the pool slightly longer than it was possible to hold my breath. The terror began to scream inside me. Just short of the point where I could no longer control the gagging impulse to inhale, he pulled me slowly to the surface.

The second time down I barely had a chance for a breath, and the terror was almost immediate. Only Juapa was in no hurry. When I came to the surface sputtering, thankful to be alive, I knew Borrasa was right. It was only a matter of time. I said I'd tell them what they wanted to know, just don't send me down again.

Juapa smiled and dropped me in a final time to make sure.

When he reeled me up, I told them everything. I blabbed like a madman, the words tumbling over one another to get out.

I told them about Howard and Caleb and finally Davina. I told them about frozen-faced Coudert and his seedy mercenaries and the plan to sack the Villa Joyosa.

Borrasa and Juapa listened without comment.

"And when was this raid due to commence?"

"At four minutes past five in the morning."

Borrasa looked at his watch and frowned. "It is already ten minutes past the hour."

"The one named Caleb was supposed to blow up the launch as a signal for the raid to begin."

Borrasa blinked. "The launch?" His suntan went green. There was something he hadn't known after all.

He shouted a command to Juapa, who turned and started to run for the door.

He'd covered only half the distance when my ears gave a pop, there was a flash, followed by the crack of an explosion. The sliding glass door gave a snap, hung for a moment in one piece, then shattered.

Caleb had been late, but he had a great sense of timing.

What happened next came very quickly. I didn't see Juapa at all, until he hit me.

The yellow light exploded again, the fingers of pain going out in every direction from my face. He hit me again, I think, because my head snapped back and I nastied up Borrasa's white leather couch.

Then he left me alone, and I decided to leave my head right where it was, forever if need be. A familiar aroma caught at my nostrils, and at first I thought it was blood. It wasn't coppery, though; it was sweet. It took me a moment to recognize what it was.

Someone not long before had been sitting on Borrasa's couch, in the exact same place, perspiring in the heat of the evening. The scent of his cologne had rubbed off on the leather.

When it finally struck me, I knew then things had gone wronger than I'd even dreamed. It was the sweet, stinking scent of frangipani.

22

I was willing to admit I'd imagined it. Except frangipani isn't in the realm of things I imagine, and it was unlikely any of Borrasa's millionaire friends had bad enough taste to have worn it themselves.

The thought of Coudert a guest in Borrasa's library didn't fit what appeared to be happening.

We were halfway up the narrow stairs to the top floor, Juapa behind me prodding with his knife, when the chatter of machine-gun fire began in the distance.

He jabbed me through the door of the small room next to the one with the radios that served as his bedroom. "I come back for you," he said, as if I were something he'd promised himself. The door slammed shut, a latch snapped, and I was alone.

The room was spartan. A single high window, narrow bed, and a plain square clothes cupboard pushed against the wall opposite the window. I went to it directly and tipped it over, not worrying about noise. I pulled it to the window, climbed onto it, and eased a look around the windowframe. The brightness of the dawn made me wince.

From that vantage point I could see almost the entire sweep of the bay. I still couldn't understand it; the raid looked in full progress.

Two machine guns were firing methodically from one of the guest villas, short, sharp bursts, the sound delayed a split second in reaching me. There was a definite pattern to the shooting, firing first at the Villa Joyosa, then raking the road, then another high over the staff cottages. Not a person in sight. If Juapa and his armed guards were planning to resist, they were keeping the idea to themselves.

Just then several men in mottled combat dress emerged from the farthest guest villa. Even at that distance I could tell Coudert from the way he lorded it over the others.

Out the door behind them came Girondas and his wife, hands over head, a single man nudging them with a leveled machine pistol.

A couple of Coudert's men scampered ahead, weaving as they ran. Coudert, his man, and the Girondases climbed into a small electric car and bounced off along the road toward the second guest villa in the line, the one that housed the machine guns. I remembered Coudert saying that he intended to gather all of the guests under one roof so they'd be easier to guard.

When they reached it, Coudert led the way inside.

A moment later he and his men were out again, minus Girondas. At once one of the machine guns focused a steady stream of fire along the window tops and roof of the next villa in line. Then Coudert's men advanced.

I stuck my head a little farther out the window and looked down. No Howard or Caleb, nothing but three floors of vertical wall and below, the slope leading down to the beach. I took too long a look. Suddenly my head was caught in a wind tunnel. Bits of wood and plaster stung the back of my neck as the windowframe above my head disintegrated in a well-placed burst of machine-gun fire.

They weren't faking it, and if Coudert had visited Borrasa, they ought to have been. Coudert would have had only one purpose. To bargain with what he knew about the raid in exchange for safety and adequate monetary compensation. There had been almost three hours between the time he and his men had been landed in their small boat by Cruz and the actual beginning of the raid. It was time enough.

Of course Borrasa would have demanded proof that it wasn't all a scheme to extort something for nothing.

Which meant it was Coudert who had finked on me and thrown in my passport lifted from the farmhouse as evidence. Borrasa's questioning me had been to confirm that Coudert had told him the truth. With a plan to formulate in a hurry he had forgotten to tell Borrasa of Caleb's intention to blow the launch or had a reason to omit it.

If they had struck a bargain, then why had Coudert returned and carried on with the raid?

There was one answer. Borrasa had wanted revenge, and Howard, Caleb, and Cruz were not to be had. Not until event 26, when, according to Howard's plan, all teams assembled at the Villa Joyosa. At which point Coudert's machine pistols would be useful. With Borrasa's blessing, Coudert had gone through the motions of carrying out his part in the raid. A little more energetically than necessary, it looked to me.

I climbed off the clothes cupboard. The door to the landing was thick oak and bolted solidly. The window was forty feet above hard ground, in full sight of Coudert's machine gunners. That trapped feeling began to wrap itself around me like a cocoon, when I remembered what else I'd seen with my head stuck out the window. Another window about ten feet below and off a few feet to the left. One of the rooms on the floor below.

I didn't know if bedsheets tied together had ever really been used to climb out a window. I didn't however intend to stay where I was and wait for Juapa.

Howard and Caleb could jolly well take care of themselves.

I went to the bed, pulled back the rough blanket, and stared at a soiled bare mattress. Juapa was all man. No sheets, not even a pillow case.

I turned to the mess of stuff that had dumped from the clothes cupboard when I'd tipped it over. I picked up one of his roll-collared white shirts. It was very good quality, made of Swiss pima, from an expensive store on the Via Veneto and bought by the dozen. I twisted the shirt around the doorknob, pulled, and found it wouldn't tear easily.

For added strength I tore loose some wire that came through the wall from the radio room and attached to a blinker-buzzer gizmo that alerted Juapa to incoming radio transmissions.

It took me a long five minutes to knot a half dozen of Juapa's shirts into a rope of sorts, and spiral the wire around it. I'd just finished when I heard a shotgun blast from inside the villa, followed by an almost immediate pair of quick single shots from someone's machine pistol. Howard and Caleb at work. I thought about hammering on the door but decided I'd only get Juapa sooner than I expected.

I climbed onto the cupboard again and looked out more cautiously this time.

Coudert and five of his men were coming along the stone-paved road now, toward the Villa Joyosa, in two electric carts. Coudert carried a pistol in one hand, a gray canvas sack with the collected loot in the other. One man had stayed behind to guard the guests.

I waited until Coudert and his men had abandoned the carts.

One party of three came upslope, intending to enter the back of the villa, no doubt, machine pistols at the ready. Coudert and two other men went through the boathouse. A dull rumble signified they were ascending via the cable car. At almost the same moment a dull crump of an explosion shook the entire villa. Caleb had blown the safe. The rest of it would happen very soon.

I began working in a frenzy then. I tied my makeshift rope to the leg of the clothes cupboard and threw the other end out the window.

I waited a split second to see if man number six was covering the Villa Joyosa over the sights of one of the machine guns. When nothing happened, I pulled the rope back in, stuck it through my belt making a loop, and tossed it out again. I straddled the window ledge, took a deep breath, and put a foot out into space.

The knots I'd made in the shirt were too big to slip easily around my belt, and it took several minutes to lower myself to the window below. I was almost level with it when man number six woke up. I heard the smack of bullets strike high and to my right, chewing up plaster and white paint. Then short, competent bursts began to work down the wall toward me.

Until then I'd forced myself to go easy, avoiding any jerky movements that might put unnecessary strain on the rope. I couldn't afford any more caution. I boosted myself away from the wall with my knees, swung out, and caught the window ledge with my foot.

My momentum was pulling me away again, like the swing of a pendulum, when a hand reached through the window and caught my ankle. About a yard in front of the sweep of machine-gun fire, I legged my way through the second-floor window and pitched forward onto a soft, luxurious carpet.

"Sammy, you look like the dogs have been at you."

Davina stood looking down at me, smiling, as though I were an old friend who had just stopped by for tea.

23

"You poor dear. Your face is a mess."

"If you want, I'll let you take part credit."

I went straight past Davina, across the room to the door. I listened and heard nothing but a silence which had grown suddenly ominous. I turned the doorknob, pulled and when nothing happened pulled harder with both hands.

"Forget it, Sammy. It's locked from the outside."

Begay luck running true as an arrow; the room with the padlock on the door, near Borrasa's library.

I hadn't looked around until then. A big room, thick white carpet, heavy white drapes, and a canopied bed with too many frills for most men to be happy with.

"Sylvia's bedroom," I said.

"Borrasa kept her almost a prisoner," said Davina. "That was my special job, Sammy. To get Sylvia. I used the rope to climb up here."

"Kidnap Borrasa's wife?"

"Lord, no. She's in it with us."

I remembered Sylvia's big fat wink, one conspirator's sign to another, if I'd been able to recognize it.

"She wanted a new chef to begin with, don't forget. The layout of the villa, the safe, all from Sylvia and mentioned innocently in letters she wrote to her mother."

"Let me guess. The crone at the farmhouse, Señora Muñoz."

Davina nodded. "Cruz is Sylvia's brother. Here, let me clean you up."

Davina found her handbag, took out a clean hankie, wetted it in a basin, and began dabbing my face. Davina was like that, bringing along her handbag. If the world were ending, she'd want to make sure she had her lipstick.

"Nice people," I said, trying to gather my thoughts. "Marry off a daughter for a few bits of information."

"Sylvia hasn't even slept with the old lech. Señora Muñoz plans to have the marriage annulled. And there won't be any evidence to prove Sylvia was actually involved. They'd have done worse if necessary, to even things with Borrasa."

"For what? And stop poking me."

"Sylvia's father and Borrasa were partners. Iron mines in the Sierra. When Muñoz died, papers were suddenly found that left the entire business to Borrasa. Against Borrasa's legal muscle the Muñozes never had a chance. Until Borrasa added the crowning insult of beginning to court Sylvia. Sylvia didn't want any part of it, but the more she put him down, the more obsessed Borrasa became. Just like a man." She stood back and looked at her handiwork. "It took Howard to see the possibilities."

"He is thorough, isn't he, Davina?"

She frowned. "He and Cruz planned most of it in prison. Borrasa had his bodyguard, Juapa, provoke Cruz into a fight that ended up with Cruz in jail, to keep him from interfering with Borrasa's formal courting of Sylvia."

"Howard figured every angle."

"Of course, he thinks of everything."

"Then why was he in prison?"

Davina flushed. "Howard believes Europe is wide open for all kinds of American know-how...."

"Davina!"

"He was caught smuggling gold sovereigns into Spain from Ceuta."

"Gold sovereigns?" I couldn't believe it.

"They weren't real."

"Counterfeit gold coins. Nobody thought of that until the Romans."

"Don't be nasty."

"The big-timers, the ones who never fail."

"That was before Howard came to Caleb. Besides, Caleb says you can't learn without making a few mistakes."

"Good for Caleb. Howard is going to learn enough today to last him a lifetime. Which may be very short."

"What do you mean?"

When I told her that Coudert had made a deal with Borrasa, she just looked at me.

I was on my feet, pacing. "Now, Davina, all I want to hear is one thing. That Howard and Caleb figured Coudert was devious enough to think about a double cross."

"They thought he might." She said it very quietly.

"Then they worked out the probablies for Coudert just like they did for me. They anticipated everything. And they're ready for him. Tell me that, Davina."

Her head began swinging from side to side.

"Oh, nuts," I said.

"Not a deal with Borrasa, nothing here. They thought Coudert would wait until we reached the mainland with the jewels. He wasn't going to get that far." She looked at me, the comprehension finally taking hold. "Coudert will catch them hanging out. Oh, Howard. . . ."

Almost as if Davina's words had been a premonition, three shots, close together, rang out below in the villa. Davina for the first time began to look frightened.

"You should have got out while you had the chance," I said, softly. "Given Borrasa's encouragement, Juapa will dream up some very special games for the lot of us."

She watched me wide-eyed. "I tried. After I used the rope to get in here and lower Sylvia, I started out behind her but heard people on the road."

"Probably Coudert leaving."

"When I started out a second time, there were guards under the window with flashlights. I thought they were looking for Sylvia."

"They were looking for me. The last time I saw Sylvia she was snug in our bed."

"She must have got frightened by the same people who spooked me. We were supposed to go straight to the boathouse and hide aboard the *Sylvia*."

"The *Sylvia*?"

Davina nodded. "Caleb blew the launch so the *Sylvia* would be the only boat left. We were going to use it to escape."

"What about the boats Cruz brought over?"

"He sank them after he landed Coudert and his men, Caleb, and Howard."

"Coudert was supposed to return to his boat after the raid, for transport back to the mainland." Davina's eyes wandered. "That what you meant about not getting that far? He'd have found his boat underwater."

"Coudert was expendable," she said, with sudden iciness.

"And who else?"

She looked up quickly. "You were coming with us, Sammy. Honest."

"It doesn't matter. We're stuck. Those gunshots mean Borrasa has Howard and Caleb prisoner." Or worse, I could have added.

"We can use the rope to get out of here, Sammy. We've got to save them."

"I can't run in the door and say boo."

"Then we'll need help."

"Davina, everyone on this island except the guests Coudert herded together is right downstairs, and not a friend among them."

"Sammy, we have to try."

If I'd even had half a notion how to pilot the *Sylvia* myself, I'd have told her why I didn't have to do anything for Howard. And there was still the diamond.

"Sammy?" Davina said slowly. "If Coudert made a deal with Borrasa, why did he really have to take Borrasa's guests prisoner? And the canvas bag I saw him carrying was bulging."

There was a very good reason, I realized. By making a deal with Borrasa, Coudert had neatly insured against any unforeseen dangers in the raid. But once he and his men controlled the situation at gunpoint, there was nothing to prevent him from double crossing both Howard and Borrasa, gathering everything he could carry and making a hasty exit.

"All right, I have an idea." I went straight to Sylvia Borrasa's dressing table and began poking through the drawers.

"Sammy, what are you doing!"

"We'll try to liberate Borrasa's guests and use them to spring Howard and Caleb. But we've got to hurry, before Coudert and his men pack up and leave."

"Quit feeling her underwear."

"I need socks," I said. "My feet are raw. You get busy and anchor that rope to something solid. We'll have to chance the window."

I wanted something else, too. If opportunity presented itself, I, for once, intended to be ready.

I found the Frederika Diamond Sylvia had worn at the banquet tossed carelessly into the top drawer of the dressing table. If there was anything in its sparkle to indicate whether it was the real diamond or the paste copy, I couldn't divine it. But if Sylvia had access to the real stone, I reasoned, we wouldn't have needed to go through this drill.

I slipped the stone into its chamois pouch, zipped it shut, and put the pouch into my pocket.

When Davina had knotted the rope to the iron window latch, she turned. "Done." She scooped up her handbag and stood next to the window, watching me anxiously.

From among Sylvia's silky underthings I separated a couple of pairs of nylon stockings. I trimmed them off quickly with manicure scissors and pulled them on.

I hadn't been fooling about my feet. When Juapa had burst in, I'd only had time for shoes. I was blistered and sore, and I wasn't one of those European playboys who can walk about in loafers without socks on.

"What about the machine gun?"

"Only one guard is watching the guests. He didn't

notice me until I'd been dangling out the window several minutes. He probably has his hands full. We'd better hope so."

"We've got to hurry, Sammy."

There was something in the way she said it. I'd heard that tone before.

"Davina, what else is there I don't know?"

She hesitated, chewing the tip of her tongue. "The *guardia civil*."

"The *guardia civil*?"

"Uh-huh. Señora Muñoz telephoned them at exactly five this morning and told them everything that was happening on Tiburón."

"But why?"

"To catch Coudert and his men red-handed, of course. Howard said it would solve a lot of problems." Davina glanced at her watch. "They should arrive just about now."

24

"Oh, Sergeant Klug, thank God," sighed Davina.

The big lump of a man I remembered from Howard's briefing leaned against the doorframe of the guest villa, sipping at a mug. A machine pistol cradled loosely in the crook of an arm.

The idea had been Davina's, and it might have worked if Klug had been as slow-witted as he looked.

He looked up at the sound of her voice. I could tell, for a minute, he wasn't sure.

Davina had come weaving around one corner of the guest villa, blouse torn to reveal a bare shoulder and a good deal more. Her honey-colored hair hung freely, all giving the impression she'd been treated more than impolitely.

She thanked God and Sergeant Klug once again and started toward him unsteadily, her arms outstretched as though pleading for some big, strong man to help her before she collapsed. When he did, I would do my part.

We'd discovered coming down the slope behind the guest villa that it hadn't been assigned to anyone owing to its current use as a storehouse. The half-ton Land Rover was pulled in beneath the overhang, as were a dozen or so bags of fertilizer and an assortment of garden tools. While Davina had made her way around the villa to attract Klug's attention, I chose a rake handle and crept to the opposite corner of the villa to wait. When Klug left the doorway to aid Davina, she was to grab him in a bear hug, I would rush forward with the rake handle, and that would be that.

"You better hit him hard," Davina had warned, "or you'll be sorry."

Like all Williamson plans, it hinged on human weakness and was intended to be executed without mercy.

Klug stepped clear of the doorway, staring at Davina uncertainly. She was nearly to him when he put down the mug and raised the machine pistol.

"Halt," he said, pointing the weapon directly at her heaving bosom.

She staggered another step, but stopped dead when Klug clicked off the safety.

"I don't like stupid tricks," said Sergeant Klug.

He gestured her toward the doorway of the guest villa. Davina had been cocksure Klug would go for her lady-in-distress act. And there had been a reasonable chance Coudert had neglected to tell his men that Davina and I were now to be considered the enemy. Wrong on both counts. I stood there, rake handle in hand, hiding behind the corner of the villa while Klug marched Davina inside, a prisoner.

If he locked himself in, there wasn't a chance of taking him alone. I needed the manpower inside.

When Klug had his back toward me, going through the door, I moved. Desperation is often mistaken for courage, I think.

I went through the doorway behind him. He was turning at the sound when I swung the rake handle at the machine pistol. I caught the protruding magazine, sending the gun out of Klug's hands and across the floor, my weapon along with it.

Me and one very startled Klug stood facing one another bare-handed.

Davina let out a whoop and grabbed him from behind, her arms pinching around his ample middle.

"Hit him!" Davina screamed.

"With what?" Klug was grappling for an evil-looking combat knife on his belt.

"Your fist," Davina wailed again.

I took a step forward and threw everything I had behind a punch worthy of the movie greats. A jaw I've found out since is a more solid piece of bone than most hands, especially hit square on. Someone plugged my fist into a light socket. Current went up my arm and down again, and there was a yell I hated to admit was my own. My right hand was suddenly without feeling.

"Again, Sammy!"

I tried a left that crossed Klug's jaw with an ugly hollow crack. His eyes went filmy. When his knees buckled, Davina let loose. Halfway down Klug's knees caught, and his hand came up with the knife in it.

He was lunging toward me when Davina nailed him with the only thing close by, a pottery ornamental horse. It splintered in a hundred pieces over Klug's head, but he crumpled and stayed down.

Coudert's men had used adhesive tape in large quantities to secure Girondas, Falek, the Swiss banker Schiller, and their wives. He'd been gentlemanly enough to allow the ladies use of the bed.

They were laid out side by side, adhesive tape wound around their heads across their mouths and hair. Caught in the middle of the night without benefit of makeup, they were a tired-looking lot, but still capable of an outraged hum. The men were on the floor bound securely in fetal position.

I used Klug's knife to cut loose Girondas first. He looked the angriest.

"Nazi pig," Girondas spat, staring at prostrate Klug. I'd cut loose his hands and had been working on his feet when Girondas tore the adhesive tape from his face, without so much as a wince.

When he was free, he jumped to his feet, snatched the machine pistol from the floor, and took charge.

I told him who I was before he could ask.

"The chef?" He studied me for a moment.

"We were lucky to escape. The thugs are looting the villa."

I started toward the bed when Girondas grabbed me roughly by the arm. "Forget the women. I need men."

He stomped around the room like an angry bull, while I freed Mahmoud Falek.

Klug was conscious by this time, trying to struggle to his feet. Girondas waited until the precise moment, then kicked his legs out from under him and sent him sprawling.

He bent his face close to Klug and muttered something in gutter German. Whatever he said, Klug went pale and didn't try to get up again.

"Nazi scum," crowed Girondas. "In second war, I chase Nazi scum from Piraeus to Kirkira."

Nikolides Girondas was a frightening little man.

Falek stood up and gave me a liquid grin. For a moment I wondered why, until his feminine eyes wandered down my body and stopped at my feet. I looked down. One of Sylvia Moñoz Borrasa's nylon stockings had fallen around my ankle. Falek smiled again, and I guessed he must have liked to dress up a little himself.

When I cut Schiller loose, he sighed as though it were all he was capable of. Close up, his luminous skin looked nearly transparent.

"Now we go," said Girondas impatiently. I'd been ready to suggest the idea of aiding those in the villa, but Girondas was way ahead of me. He was no longer bored; he was hungry for action.

He handed the machine pistol to a startled Falek, bound Klug, and marched straight to one of the machine guns.

He studied it for a moment. Then with quick decisive movements he pulled out a pin, wrestled the heavy gun from its four-legged mount, and carried it toward the door.

"This in Land Rover, we give the scum a good time, eh?"

"Perhaps I'd best attend the ladies," said Schiller.

Girondas looked at him darkly.

Just like a bloody Swiss. A fight was coming, and Schiller intended to remain neutral.

"I can't shoot this," whined Falek, staring at the machine pistol. "I don't know how." He was almost relieved.

"Then you drive. Every Arab can drive." There was an authority in Girondas' tone that didn't allow argument.

Falek sighed and nodded.

"Give that to him," Girondas said, indicating me. He came over to me and grinned. "You a very brave boy. You and I shoot the guns, eh?"

In the end it was Falek's driving that allowed Davina and me to remove ourselves from the Girondas war party.

Girondas dropped the windshield on the Land Rover and propped the machine-gun mount across the hood. He used sacks of fertilizer to shore up the mount and set in the machine gun. "Like sandbags, eh?" He worked like a man possessed.

He fed a belt of ammunition into the gun, jerked back a lever on one side, and gave the barrel a couple of tentative swings.

"Ready," he pronounced, and looked at the rest of us.

Falek gave me a pleading glance but climbed behind the wheel when Girondas glared at him. I gave Davina a hand up into the back, Girondas too preoccupied playing with his machine gun to offer an objection.

Falek whispered to Allah to grace him quickly with baraka and pressed the starter.

"Use the choke, Arab," yelled Girondas, and added threateningly: "You drive good or you emigrate to Brazil."

The engine turned over, caught, ran roughly for a moment, then smoothed out. Falek ground the Land Rover into gear and ran it down from beneath the overhang and turned reluctantly along the road toward the Villa Joyosa.

I don't know if Girondas had a plan, but people with his sort of bull aggressiveness always seem to get what they want.

We were still a hundred yards from the Villa Joyosa when Coudert and his men came around one corner.

They were moving fast down the slope of the hill, not expecting trouble and completely oblivious of us approaching from their blind side. They were heading directly toward the boathouse and the *Sylvia*. When Coudert went through the boathouse earlier on his way to the cable car, he must have noted it was intact. He was no dummy.

Girondas waited until they were midway down the hill framed against the bare wall of the villa before he fired. It was a difficult shot, upslope from a moving vehicle, or Girondas would have shot them down like clay targets. As it was the first shots struck over their heads, the bullets slanting still higher up the wall as he continued to fire.

At the sound of the machine gun both Davina and I jumped a mile. The loudness of it must have startled Falek too, for even before Girondas could fire another burst, the Land Rover jolted to the right, dropping its right front wheel off the edge of the road.

Girondas called Falek a turd in Greek and stood up, adjusting his stance to the tilt of the vehicle. He fired quickly, but by then Coudert's men had spread like so many quail.

Most followed their inclination and the slope of the land and pitched ahead down the hill. But not Coudert. With the sound of the first shot he had dropped into a crouch. I saw him hesitate, letting his men run past him, drawing attention. Then, still clutching the gray sack to his chest, he spun around and sprinted back up the hill toward the villa.

The ploy didn't fool Girondas. He let out a satisfied grunt and swung the barrel of the machine gun toward Coudert. Falek, twisting the wheel of the Land Rover, brought it back onto the road at the precise instant Girondas fired. Coudert had nearly reached the corner of the villa when machine-gun bullets kicked up great plumes of dust behind him. When the dust cleared, he was gone.

I thought for a minute Girondas would turn the gun on Falek. He let out a childlike cry of frustration and swung the heavy gun back toward Coudert's men, who by then had rounded the bottom of the villa and were moving almost directly away, darting and weaving as they ran, not even bothering to return fire. They were heading now, no doubt, for the point where they thought the small boat they had landed in would be waiting.

Logic said Coudert would do the same. The sight of Coudert running for his life would have satisfied me perfectly as a final glimpse of the good major. It was too much to hope for.

Whether Girondas or the *guardia civil* caught the lot of them first I didn't care. In the moment Falek had stalled the Land Rover I grabbed Davina by the arm, and together we went over the tailgate.

We were a good thirty feet from the Land Rover before Girondas spotted us. When he did, he spun around and yelled angrily. "You running away, you scum."

"Help," I said, pointing toward the villa. "Going to get help."

He grinned suddenly and gave Falek a mean slap on the shoulder. "Go, Arab."

Girondas was already hunched over the machine gun firing as Falek drove the Land Rover off in the direction of Coudert's retreating troopers. I'm pleased to say I've never seen either of them again.

25

"What took you so long, boy?" Caleb said, when I tore off the adhesive tape. If his color hadn't been slate gray, an ugly welt on his forehead, I'd have taken my time.

We found almost everyone in the dining room bound with adhesive tape, lined up against one wall like plaster of Paris monkeys all in a row. Borrasa's eyes followed me angrily, and he tried to say something through the adhesive tape; I left him where he was.

A blast from a shotgun had taken off one leg of the dining-room table, and the place stank of burned explosive. Someone was moaning, more a hurt whimper than the agonies of death. It wasn't until I'd untied Caleb that I saw it was Juapa.

He sat dazed and awkward against the wall, one arm hanging loose.

"What happened to him?"

"He came at me with a knife," said Caleb, "so I applied my patented anti-knife-wielder defense."

"What's that?"

"I shot the bastard."

The thought of the shots I'd heard actually shedding somebody's blood, even Juapa's, made the scene suddenly ugly.

"I'd have made a decent job of it," Caleb added, "if it hadn't been for my buddy Coudert."

"What about Coudert?" asked Howard, standing, rubbing his wrists nervously. Not even a thank-you and congratulations. Our arrival might have been according to plan.

"He was headed for the *Sylvia*," I said. "Girondas commandeered the Land Rover and a machine gun and made him change his mind. Coudert's men were last seen going east. I don't know what happened to Coudert."

Howard gazed thoughtfully at the wall for a moment. Then took the machine pistol from me, checked the magazine, and cocked it.

"Sammy, where's the knife?" Davina was picking unsuccessfully at the adhesive tape that bound Cruz.

"I didn't bring it. I'll get one from the kitchen."

"You better not go in there," Howard said quietly.

I turned around and looked at him. "Why?"

"It would be better if you didn't."

Caleb said, "Coudert shot one of Borrasa's people while he was locking the household staff in a kitchen cupboard. One of them didn't like the idea."

Davina looked up. "Who?"

"One of the cooks," said Caleb.

Davina shut her eyes. "Oh, Sammy."

"There was only one. It was his kitchen!"

Whatever else was said to me I didn't hear. I ran down the short hall and pushed open the kitchen door.

Vasco Ibarra lay on his back on the kitchen floor, among strewn pots and pans, his sad eyes open wide in surprise. Three dark holes you could have covered with a playing card were in the middle of his white tunic. The blood had spread out around him, a solid stain almost a yard across. I had no idea a human body carried so much of it, even one as small as Vasco. I'd never seen anyone who had died violently before. It sickened me, not physically, but that anyone could insult a human being with such an absurd, obscene ending to his time on earth.

I don't know how long I stood there, staring down at poor Vasco. The next thing I knew Howard was there next to me.

"Come on, Sammy," he said brusquely, "the others are aboard the *Sylvia*. We're not out of this yet."

"You and your bloody plan. The whole bloody thing was a waste."

Someone began pounding on the door of the larder from inside.

Howard looked up, jumpily. "I'm sorry about him, but that's the breaks. We came here to do a job with risks, and we did it."

"You got Vasco killed and let Coudert run off with the prize. That's what you mean."

"Coudert took the hundred thousand Swiss francs we found in the safe and the diamonds belonging to Falek and Girondas." Howard smiled thinly. "And a Picasso, a small etching of an unhappy clown."

"Coudert's all heart."

"He left the diamond." Howard took a small chamois bag from his pocket identical to the one I had with the paste stone in it and held it up, smiling. "This, and Señora Schiller's emerald tiara, and a considerable number of objects of art. He didn't want them evidently. Without contacts they'd be more trouble to fence than they're worth, and I imagine the major intends to remain mobile. Now come along." He skirted Vasco's body carefully, avoiding the pool of blood. "We must send the widow flowers."

The airy way he said it made me understand, finally, what an icy bastard Howard was.

The pounding came again from inside the larder, and I started toward the door.

"Leave them, Sammy. We don't have time."

I spun on him. "I will not leave them. I'm not going to leave Vasco's brigade, my brigade, in any larder like a bunch of green chilies."

Howard stared at me but didn't say a word.

There were half a dozen of the household staff locked inside, including Mrs. Vasco, Florita and crazy Juan.

When I let them out, Vasco's wife gave a mournful wail and flopped down across Vasco's body. Florita dabbed a handkerchief in the blood on the floor and crossed herself, her eyes saucer-wide.

When old Juan started grinning at me, I turned away and followed Howard out the rear door of the kitchen and didn't look back.

26

We were still fifty feet from the boathouse when Howard stopped.

The deep rumble of a pair of marine engines was clearly audible inside. The breeze had quit, and the air was oppressive and still.

"What's wrong?"

"Shhh." Howard brought the machine pistol up. We were tight against the side of the Villa Joyosa, the pebbled fringe of beach still a few feet ahead. I tried to follow his gaze from the boathouse, upward along the cable car rails past the gatehouse at the patio. The rails disappeared above us. The cable car must have been at the top, stopped at the terrace of Borrasa's library. "I thought I heard something." He shook his head. "We'll be in the open crossing the beach. We'd better go one at a time."

"No deal."

Howard smiled. "You still don't trust me, do you?"

"I never did."

"I didn't have to come back to the kitchen for you, Samuel. I could have gone with the others to the *Sylvia* and left you for Coudert or the *guardia civil*. I had no intention of leaving you here."

"Then why did you clonk me on the head and dump me on Borrasa's doorstep?"

"I was afraid with everything about to happen you'd be injured. You were safer with Borrasa. Of course, I didn't know then of Coudert's deception." Before I could question it, he said, "I'll go first. You cover me."

He held out the machine pistol.

"I wouldn't know what to do with it."

"It's quite simple. This is a Sterling Patchett Mark 111. Thirty rounds, cyclic rate of fire—"

I cut him off. "You've never shot one either, Howard. It's the raid all over again, isn't it? All theory."

He grinned, boyishly. "I have it on good authority a novice can achieve thirty-inch groups at twenty-five yards. When fired, it climbs up and to the left. Remember that."

"You remember it. You keep the gun. For security, I'll hang onto the diamond."

Howard looked at me a second, measuring. "Fair enough." He handed me the chamois pouch. By his reckoning there was no risk to it.

He straightened and began to trot across the beach toward the entrance to the boathouse.

I waited until he was halfway before I dug around in the pebbles at the edge of the beach and found one the right size.

Howard had almost reached the boathouse door when Coudert shot him.

I wasn't sure at first what happened. Howard appeared to stumble, but then kept going forward, the machine pistol whirling away behind him, when he made an awkward grab at his pelvis.

I barely heard the shot over the sound of the *Sylvia*'s engines. Then from somewhere above I heard Coudert's laughter, without mistake. It wasn't until the cable car clanked into gear and began descending that I could pinpoint him exactly.

He'd been hiding on the terrace. He must have doubled back through the villa after being shot at by Girondas, still hoping to escape aboard the *Sylvia*. The others had gone aboard before he could try it, and he'd hidden and waited for whoever else was to come. From Coudert's position he wouldn't have seen Howard until he'd started across the beach, which meant he hadn't seen me at all.

I looked across at Howard sitting in the sand. He was

watching the scarlet stain spread out around him as though he couldn't understand how it happened. He reached toward the machine pistol, but it was a yard away.

"I wouldn't try, Williamson," said Coudert. "At least now you're likely to live. Your life is fair exchange for transport to the mainland, isn't it?"

Howard tried to speak, but it must have hurt too much. His eyes followed Coudert's slow descent in the cable car, then slid directly toward me.

He must have been out of his mind. I was hidden from Coudert's view, and Coudert was armed. I had the Frederika Diamond. All I had to do was hike off and hide in the hills until the *guardia civil* had come and gone, then figure a way to cross the channel between Tiburón and the mainland. I'd be a couple of million richer even if I had to swim. Howard was crazy. His eyes dropped from mine and rested directly on the machine pistol.

The cable car came into view then, and I could see Coudert. It was midway between the terrace and the patio gatehouse, where Vasco had greeted Davina and me the first day. A pistol cradled in Coudert's hands, aimed steadily at Howard. Howard was his ticket out, and he wasn't going to lose it.

I thought Coudert had forgotten my existence until he spoke. He'd have been smarter to keep his mouth shut.

"I'm afraid we'll have to leave your lackey behind. I hope the thought doesn't sadden you, Williamson."

"You mean Begay?"

From the way his face contorted you could see it took Howard some grit to get it out. He wanted to make sure I understood. I was the lackey.

"Begay?" Coudert pronounced my name with rising inflection, as if it were some joke. "Yes, Begay," he repeated, the laughter that followed biting away at me like the edge of a saw.

It was a laughter I'd heard before. From T. I. T. Quinn and Neil and Juapa and how many others I couldn't have said. A laugh with no fun in it, of one person telling you in the most arrogant possible way that he has the power. Your balls in the vise, his hand on the screw, and you can bet he's going to give it a turn. I'd been hearing that laughter all my bloody life. I didn't intend hearing it ever again.

I looked up at Coudert and wondered if there had been laughter before he'd shot down helpless Vasco.

The cable car was almost to the small gatehouse at the patio. For the few seconds it took to pass through, Coudert's view of the beach would be blocked by the walls of the gatehouse itself. It wasn't really enough time.

Coudert's laughter was still in my ears when I found myself running, forcing out every thought except reaching the machine pistol in the sand.

When my hands had closed around it I remember a shot, and the sound of a freight train rushing by my head. I pointed the machine pistol toward Coudert's laughter and pulled the trigger, feeling it suddenly alive in my grip.

When I could see clearly again, the cable car had stopped several feet beyond the gatehouse. The metal siding covering the lower half had more holes in it than I could count.

I didn't see Coudert, and to this day I don't know if I am a murderer. If so, I haven't the slightest remorse.

I dropped the machine pistol and pulled Howard to his feet, ignoring his yelp. I put him over my shoulder, and if he was heavy I didn t notice it. Then I carried him aboard the *Sylvia*.

27

When the *Sylvia* hit the open sea, Cruz at the wheel, I went straight into the toilet. While Davina and Caleb attended to Howard, I'd waited only until I'd spotted Davina's handbag.

Among other things I was sick to my stomach more from the events of the past few hours catching up than from seasickness. But I didn't remain in the toilet longer than necessary.

When I was finished, I hesitated a moment and stared at the face in the small mirror I hardly recognized as my own, hoping for a sign whether my run of luck was going to hold. Once I walked back into the cabin, I was committed. As usual when you really need a sign, you're sure not to get it. I took another look at the face and thought it a little different somehow. "Press it," I said to the face, and walked out through the door.

Everyone was still clustered around Howard, lying on the galley table on his stomach. One of Cruz's men had retrieved the canvas bag from the cable car, and Howard hugged it as a chin rest. Color was back in his face, no doubt from its closeness to all that loot.

Coudert's bullet had put a furrow along his left hip. With his skivvies down around his knees Howard gritted his teeth, more embarrassed than pained. Davina bandaged the wound with strips of towel, while Sylvia Borrasa patted his forehead with a damp cloth, in a tender way Howard should have paid more attention to.

When Davina finished, he grinned up at me and held out his hand.

"The diamond, Samuel. I'll take it back now."

I dropped the chamois pouch into his hand and looked up to see Caleb eyeing the transaction narrowly over the top of a mug of bourbon.

If Caleb picked that moment to examine what was in the chamois pouch, I'd have some awkward, very rapid explaining to do. He didn't. He looked at Howard, waiting to see what he would do. When Howard dropped the pouch into the canvas bag with nary more than a squeeze, Caleb took a slow, thoughtful sip of bourbon, to hide a half-smile.

The rest of the trip he divided his time between watching the stretch of water toward the mainland for some sign of the much-overdue *guardia civil* and staring at me with that half-smile. My face didn't give up a twitch.

Cruz grounded the *Sylvia* in a quiet sandy cove on the coast west of La Boca.

Señora Muñoz was waiting with the Renault 16 and an old Bedford van. We separated there, Cruz giving Howard a quick *abrazo*, like the pair of thick thieves they were.

Sylvia Borrasa, or Muñoz as it would soon be again, glared at me, unforgiving of the pat I'd given her in bed. She gave Howard a hot, pouty look before the Muñozes drove off in the van. I've seen the look Latin women get when they make up their minds about something. With what I'd seen of Sylvia's temper, it would serve Howard right.

The rest of us set off east in the Renault.

Where the road from La Boca joined the Málaga-Almeria highway, we hit traffic crawling at a snail's pace around an accident. Off to one side a big olive-drab, military ten-wheeler had struck a truck full of chickens. Lots of blood and feathers, and men in uniform arguing, but among the bodies nothing I recognized as human.

On the door of the ten-wheeler were lettered the two words, *guardia civil*. Davina rolled her eyes at me; Howard for once had no comment.

We were closer to Almeria than I expected before

Caleb pulled the Renault off the highway onto a side road and stopped.

There was a long moment before Howard said, "Well, Samuel, I'm afraid we part company here."

Davina looked straight ahead. Caleb shook his head as though it were the saddest thing that had ever happened to him.

"What do you mean?"

"I mean we've a plane to catch and reservations for three. You can wave down a bus along the highway."

I didn't move. "This was the idea all along."

"No, but I lied to you. We did intend to leave you behind with Coudert, which is why I knocked you unconscious. But you've been helpful. I want to show my appreciation. You have your safety now, so if you'll step out of the car we'll call it even."

"No," said Davina. She glared at Howard, her jaw clamped defiantly.

Caleb made a clucking sound. "Now, Davina honey. . . ."

"Don't honey me, Caleb. It's dirty and rotten, and it isn't fair. If it hadn't been for Sammy, you'd both be dead or in jail."

"It's a hard world," said Howard. "All right, Samuel, out." He pointed a pistol at me.

"If he goes, so do I," said Davina. She looked at me softly. "That's if you want me, Sammy."

It was one of those points of decision. "Sure," I said.

"You don't sound sure."

"I mean yes."

Howard said, "Don't be foolish, Davina."

"I'd be more than foolish if I lived the rest of my life with you two. No thanks."

"Let her go, Howard," Caleb said coldly. "She never did have any sense about men. It might learn her something."

Davina gave a wounded moan and stepped out of the car. "I hope Borrasa catches both of you. You stink."

"Davina, reconsider." Howard had as much emotion in his voice as I remember. "Please."

"Come on, Sammy," Davina said, taking my hand. "We're going to do just fine."

When the car had left us standing in the road, Davina clutching her handbag, me with little more than the clothes on my back, we both began to laugh. It was the happiest laughter I'd ever heard.

We caught a bus to Almería and found a clean little hotel near the ocean. I mentioned my affiliation with the house of Borrasa to get us a room with a sea view and private bath without benefit of luggage. I asked the concierge to send up a bottle of sparkling wine.

"What's the occasion?" asked Davina. We drank half the bottle before I opened her handbag and dug out the chamois pouch.

"This."

"Sammy," she said, staring at the stone I took from the pouch. Then it dawned. "Oh, Sammy."

She did a dance around the room with me that brought back the nausea.

I excused myself, went into the bathroom, inspected it carefully, then peeled myself down to the skin. When I was finished, I climbed beneath the shower and washed off the dirt and dust of Borrasa's island.

Finished, I wrapped a towel around myself, hesitated a moment at the bathroom door, took a deep breath, and opened it.

Davina was sitting on the bed staring at the stone, a distant, satisfied grin parting her full lips.

"You put the diamond in my purse because you knew I'd come with you."

"I thought you might."

"Cocky thing," she smiled. "What if I hadn't?" Her voice held a taunt.

"Then it wouldn't have mattered."

"That's a lot of stuff," Davina chided, "but it's nice for a girl to hear." She unsnapped her hair clip and shook her hair loose. "What was in the pouch you gave Howard?"

"A little something I picked up."

She shook her head, still not seeming able to believe it. "You outsmarted Howard and Caleb, Sammy. You really did it." Her voice was full of pride.

"Some pussycat," I grinned.

"My pussycat."

Later in bed Davina's urgency got the better of my exhaustion, and off we went into the whirlpool. Some time after that Davina whispered, "It's going to be a good life." I remember clearly because they were the last words I'd ever hear Davina say.

When I woke up the next morning, she and the diamond were gone.

There was no hurry about getting out of bed. I ached all over, inside and out. From where I was I could see the note she'd left lipsticked on the mirror above the dresser in a scrawl like a child's.

"Dear Sammy (my pussycat)" it began. "Howard finally peeked. He thought you hid the diamond someplace (Caleb said you should have) and me coming with you was the only sure way to find out where. Sorry, darling, but no cigar. Luv'ya." It was signed "Davina."

I called down to the desk and ordered black coffee and a bottle of Carlos Primero and asked them to send up someone who could look into a plugged drain.

Fifteen minutes after a waiter brought coffee and the brandy, a short man with bushy eyebrows and a bushier mustache, waxed at the ends, arrived with a box of tools. I had him take the U-joint off the bottom of the bathroom basin, and fished out the Frederika Diamond.

In the head aboard the *Sylvia* I'd taken the real stone, put it into one of Sylvia Borrasa's nylon stockings, and tied it around my thigh tight against my groin. I'd considered placing it in the tried-and-true smugglers' hiding place, but calculated if I was challenged at all, it wouldn't fool Caleb.

Then I'd taken the pebble picked from the beach and put it into the original pouch, the one I'd handed Howard. I slipped the paste diamond into Davina's handbag while everyone's concern was still Howard.

If Howard or Caleb had looked in the pouch right then, I'd have retrieved the copy from Davina's purse, with an appropriately embarrassed grin. Caleb's silly habit of letting Howard discover his own mistakes had helped.

The plumber looked at the stone in my hand covered with soap film, then at me, without expression.

"If it were real, I'd be a rich man," I said.

He glanced at my dusty clothing on a hanger by the window. "If a goat had wings, he might be an airplane."

He was still grinning when he left.

I broke the seal on the brandy and the bottle, and I climbed back into bed.

A warm, almost peaceful feeling wanted to rise up inside me. Manning Able would have said it was because I'd finally made a success of something, if turning out to be a first-rate thief counted. With all the false starts I'd made in life I suppose it did.

Staring at myself in the toilet mirror aboard the *Sylvia*, I'd made the real discovery. I realized finally in my life that I'd rather do than get done to. If I hadn't, Howard and Caleb would have walked off with everything however lucky or smart I'd been to that point.

There was a moral in there somewhere.

I took another sip from the bottle, tried to figure what it was, and owned up that the major component of the warm, soaring feeling was the brandy. I came down hard when I remembered Davina.

That bloody woman had edged her way into a part of my life that hadn't had anything in it for a long time. While she was there, I found I liked it. More than liked it. When she had come with me, I hadn't known if

Howard and Caleb had sent her or the idea was her own.

When I'd walked out of the shower and found her still there, smiling, I thought I'd won. Davina and I would ride off together into the sunset.

I don't know how long I lay there thinking how it might have turned out if we had. When I found myself wondering more about how I was going to pay the hotel bill, I knew that I never really believed we would.

I got up and dressed.

The sun was straight overhead, the Med as blue as I'd ever seen it. The breeze had shifted around toward the south and smelled clean and fresh. An omen to note, maybe. I glanced once more at the scrawl on the mirror, remembered the sweet nutty taste of a girl's lipstick on the rim of a brandy glass, and put it out of my mind.

Papa Victor said it, anyway: You can't lose what you never owned.